A Little Bird Came Calling

A Hugo Storm Crime Thriller, Volume 1

Anton Lindbak

Published by Back Close Books, 2017.

A LITTLE BIRD CAME CALLING

First edition. December 3, 2017.

Written by Anton Lindbak.

A heartfelt thank you to my Editor - D.K.T.

A further thank you to my partner in Back Close Books
for cover design and creative assistance.

This book is for you mum - wherever in Heaven you are.
Barbara Dorothy Lindbak - an English Rose - who will always be in my heart.

ONE

"I NEED MY MONEY, HUGO – that's reasonable."

The voice of Cameron Bullard was, as always, gruff but calm though not particularly hostile. That was Cameron Bullard; he would explain things in a friendly manner whilst crushing your fingers one by one with a hammer. Still, what he was saying wasn't unreasonable. The problem was, I simply couldn't give him what he wanted. I didn't have the money I owed him. Not in cash, not in any of my bank accounts. In assets yes, but it would take time to make those liquid. And it would raise questions, difficult questions, that so far, I couldn't stomach answering.

"You there, Hugo?"

The voice now had a hint of anger. Cameron Bullard wasn't the type to plea; Cameron Bullard was the type to issue commands. Still, I didn't reply, searching my thoughts frantically; what could I tell him that he hadn't heard already? I cursed myself, cursed my weakness, cursed my stupidity. The amount I owed Mr Bullard and his partners was now into six figures. They had added interest – fair enough – this was down to me. I was the fool that had got too big for my boots, lost control and gambled with money I didn't have.

"Hugo? I'm losing patience here, okay. You gotta pay or there will be consequences."

I still didn't answer – just held the phone whilst staring ahead. Unable, though, to see the way out. As a true coward I hadn't told Helena, my wife, but had used my best avoidance tactics and hoped

1

she'd never hear about it. But that was that; here and now I was searching for a way out. I wanted a cigarette. It wouldn't fix this but I needed one, even though I hadn't smoked for years. Stress had accumulated steadily over the last few months. A knock on my office door – I instantly forgot about the need for a cigarette and grabbed the opportunity to finish this call.

"Listen, Mr Bullard, I will honour my debt – just need some more time. I will get back to you." I said it quickly and terminated the call before he could reply.

Ignoring the dread forming in my stomach, I shouted, "Come in." The words came out a little angry. Cameron Bullard ran, amongst other activities, a long-standing illegal gambling venture in Edinburgh's shadow world, and one ignored him at one's peril. I knew this but forced the thought away. For now, it couldn't be helped.

"Hugo, your last appointment of the day is here."

Petite Williams, my trusted and loyal assistant, opened the door. She looked at me, and quickly and correctly diagnosed my darkened mood.

"No more calls, Hugo; you have left the office."

I looked at her and smiled. Petite Williams was a nice person and a multi-talented assistant. Her young punk look concealed a very capable operator, intelligent and savvy. This month her hair was green, and her tight-fitting black clothes only enhanced her strongly-curved womanhood.

"Sorry Petite, but yes, thank you. Please send in the client."

I said this as I took a gulp of air and cleared my head. This client would demand my full attention. I had very reluctantly accepted this appointment – only because I really needed the money. It had been a slow few months. My bank accounts were drying up. They needed refilling urgently.

"No problem, Hugo."

Petite smiled back. She was a big girl; she could handle my mood swings as a true professional. She turned to allow my new client in. Petite's look was unquestionably unorthodox, but her polite mannerisms were nothing but orthodox. A slender lady stepped into my office, dressed in black with a black silk veil over her head. She looked around before focusing on me. I immediately felt a chill emanating from her.

Chloe Cantor was a beautiful little girl, but then again weren't they all? A single child to a single mother. And by all accounts a very happy child. I remembered seeing the many photos of her smiling face in various newspapers and broadcasts. Her tanned skin and shiny black hair framed a pair of happy eyes and a wide smile. I remembered seeing those photos and genuinely feeling sorrow for the mother. How did anyone survive such emotional trauma? I felt it, being a parent myself – a father of four. I took pride in being a proper dad; a dad that was there for the rough as well as the smooth, the bad as well as the good. And now I stood face-to-face with a parent who had lost her child – a mother lost in the deep abyss – her daughter gone, and nothing left except, I guessed, the haunted elements of heart-shattering grief. Nothing had been seen or heard of Chloe Cantor, ten years, two months and five days old, when she had disappeared in a busy shopping centre in Edinburgh on Thursday 12th February 2015. I had read up on her case since her mother contacted my office a week ago. I could have seen her before, but I wanted to familiarise myself with the case. And yet, I also wanted the opportunity to chicken out and flee. To be honest, I wasn't keen on this case.

Understand this, although thousands of people go missing every year in Scotland, the majority are accounted for within 24 hours. Of those genuinely missing after that, the majority are adults who want to remain missing for whatever reason. Not many children go missing, very few in fact. When a child goes missing, it's all hands-on deck – the police throw everything they have at the case. No stone is left unturned. And this was very much the case with Chloe Cantor's disappearance. Despite a faulty start due to an arrogant Chief Inspector at the time, Police Scotland quickly got their act together. They committed everything they had in their search for little Chloe. But it didn't work out, she remained missing.

"Please Mrs Cantor, come in and have a seat."

I spoke in a gentle manner to the lady who stood as silent as a ghost in my office. As she pulled back her veil and looked at me, I saw the pain in her face. Once there had been stunning beauty there, I surmised. Once there had been laughter and happiness in that delicately sculptured, yet strong, intelligent face. Now there was only the wreckage of grief present. I knew the bottom of this mother's world had fallen out the day her little girl had vanished. Since then she had been falling deeper and deeper into the darkness. Her eyes blinked frenetically as she composed herself. How many times do you do that each day, I wondered? How many times do you take that breath, steady yourself and focus only on taking the next step, trying hard not to fall over because something tells you to keep on going? I knew this because she had come to see me. She still had some sort of hope, fragile and fractured though it was; she still hadn't given up. And that scared me – scared the living daylights out of me to be honest.

I'm a fixer, a trouble-shooter, a private investigator, and a very good one at that. I'm not bragging here, just stating a fact. But how could I deliver when the biggest police operation in modern Scottish history had failed? Although I have extensive contacts and serious resources, to all intents and purposes I was a one-man band. My skills and capabilities set me apart in modern Scottish society; even in the whole of the UK there weren't many around like me. Nonetheless, I was only one person, incapable of matching the thousands of man hours already committed by Police Scotland and other Scottish, UK and European agencies. But this was what I did; I sorted problems that others couldn't sort.

And there was more, far more to this than a mother losing her child, my instinct told me that. You didn't do what I did well without having a certain instinct that couldn't easily be quantified. One either possessed that quality or one didn't. I did. From my days in the British Army Intelligence and a successful run as a serious fraud investigator for an insurance company, I could read people and situations better than most. Not that I didn't make mistakes; failure was the flip side of the coin of success. It happened, but the crucial aspect was knowing how to deal with it when it did, that was what seeded winners from losers. I never gave up.

The lady seated herself in one of the trendy leather chairs in front of my big metal-top desk. The desk was like an aircraft carrier – big and impressive – and did what I wanted it to do: impress. Nothing attracts business more than the trappings of success. Anyway, it was stylish and practical, setting the tone in my generous-sized office. She cleared her throat and looked around again as if getting her bearings. Having regained her composure, she fixed her intense eyes upon me. I returned her gaze, and noticed again her sharp facial features and lush brown skin. Ravaged by grief, she was still very attractive. She crossed her right leg over her left, a motion I found disturbingly erotic. Her black hair was expensively cropped and her clothes, although all black, were stylish and exclusive. Very metropolitan. I took my time and studied her. She let me.

Ariella Cantor was a world-renowned art dealer of the discreet and very expensive kind. She was the type known and respected in London, New York, Paris and beyond. Her art gallery in Edinburgh was a boutique of art wealth and her opinion mattered to those in the know. She was well-connected and the more I learned about her the more intrigued I became. Ariella Cantor, the widow, seemed on a professional level at least, to be at the top of her game. Then one miserable afternoon in February her daughter disappeared, and Ariella's life fell apart. Within the next few months her life was turned upside down and inside out. The media frenzy was intense as Ariella and her daughter provided an irresistible narrative. Ariella's maiden name was Rosenstein, and she was Jewish. Born in Israel, she moved with her family to Edinburgh as a young child when her father, David Rosenstein, a banker, opened a branch of an Israeli Bank. Being a Jew, and specifically an Israeli Jew, can be a tricky issue in Scotland. Anyone from that background is frequently a prime target for hostility, especially from those at the political extremes, both left and right. By sheer association alone you become personally responsible for the conduct of the State of Israel. The only Jewish primary school in Glasgow was the only primary school in the whole of Scotland that required police protection on a regular basis. So far nothing had happened, but the underlying threat was always there – one day. And Jews worldwide, I guessed, knew that feeling by instinct – one day. So, Ariella and her fellow Scottish Israeli community had learned long ago not to broadcast their Israeli heritage. Yet after Chloe disappeared, the media reported far and wide, and there was more: gossip and rumours that must have made her daily lot a living hell. As if dealing with the trauma of losing one's child wasn't enough. A compound of mayhem.

"Does what you see correspond with what you already think, Mr Storm?" asked Ariella.

Her voice, albeit fragile and low, carried some evidence of strength. It surprised me. And I took note. There was more to Ariella Cantor than just a fractured, lost soul. Her eyes were swimming in pain, but there was a certain determination there too.

"Sorry Mrs Cantor, I don't follow," I said as I successfully managed to unglue my tongue from the roof of my mouth.

She didn't smile, just pursed her lips. Maybe she hadn't smiled once since that day in February? Maybe she had lost the ability to smile? I got that – how can you see any light in anything when your little girl is missing? Fate unknown.

"I am used to being judged by now, Mr Storm. I was just wondering about your verdict?" She said this with a portion of bitterness evident in her voice.

I shook my head. I knew where she was heading, and it was important to me for her to understand that I didn't think like that. Human perception is by its very nature, fluid and often irrational. People are quick to draw conclusions and even quicker to judge. And I knew Ariella Cantor had been through a hurricane. Outrage and sympathy had quickly changed to suspicion and hostility amongst certain elements of the public as some news providers had dug a little into the exotic life of Ariella, and had drawn hasty conclusions. But I didn't judge her on that. Carrying my fair share of secrets and battling my own demons, I couldn't help but feel a bond with this complicated human being. She had, as all of us do, just lived her life as best she could.

"No, I'm afraid I don't have a verdict, Mrs Cantor. I don't do that kind of thing," My voice was calm, but I could feel the moisture forming in the palms of my hands. This was damned hard, and if I hadn't needed the money, I would've politely declined this case by now. But I needed her money – very much so.

She looked at me again, her face suddenly locked in a spiral of grief. I guessed that happened a lot. I waited – an itch on the back of my neck was suddenly very intense. But I kept still. Let her ride it out, I told myself. Ariella got herself back. She nodded.

"Thank you, Mr Storm."

She paused, gathering strength to continue. Here we go! I was thinking as I almost gripped my desk, but managed not to – just.

"I have heard a lot about you, Mr Storm. I've done some research. You have skill sets far beyond the norm here in Scotland, even the UK. You understand, I have resources and deal with only the best, she said as she took a silver cigarette box out of her black leather handbag.

"Do you mind?" she asked.

I shook my head, "No, please go ahead. I've got an ashtray here somewhere," I replied, appreciating the opportunity to move. I got up and walked over to a large cupboard. Another stylish Nordic design, very expensive, but as I told myself when I kitted this place out, sturdy and thus long-lasting. I opened a couple of drawers before I found one, which I placed in front of the lady. She lit her cigarette and took a deep hit.

"Thank you," she said after delicately exhaling the smoke.

"Sorry, where have my manners gone? Would you like a coffee, tea or some other refreshment?" I asked as I remained standing at her side.

"No, but thank you, Mr Storm, very kind but I am fine."

She took another long hit of the cigarette, and I returned to my chair. I glanced at the wall-mounted clock behind her. It was getting late and I wanted to go home. Home to my wife and kids. And grab them all and give them a very long cuddle. She noticed, but didn't say anything. I felt a little guilty and appreciated her discreetness.

"Right, Mr Storm, I guess you know why I am here?" she asked.

"Yes," I replied simply.

I'd been debating with myself for days, about how I was going to handle this part. I am not a fragile soul, I can handle human misery and trauma quite well. But still, this one here was more difficult than any of the other cases I had ever had. Giving people hard-hitting reality checks was often part and parcel of my assignments. But, so far, none of them had involved missing kids. And there wasn't going to be a happy ending here. I suspected Ariella, despite her savoir-faire and insight, fervently hoped I could deliver the impossible: find her little girl and bring her home. And hope in this situation was dangerous, because unfulfilled, it would be devastating. But then again, did she have anything to lose? Her devastation was already complete. I decided to be honest, as honest as I could manage to be.

"You want me to search for Chloe!" Using her daughter's name made her flinch but I continued. I said 'search', not 'find' deliberately. This was important, I needed to say this even if it hurt. I took a big gulp of air and continued, "I'm sorry, Mrs Cantor but the chances of my finding Chloe are slim, I'm sorry but you need to understand that. But I promise you I'll do my very best!"

My words hit her like a heavy-weight boxer delivering blows to a punch bag. I could actually see the impact of each word hitting her in the face. But she kept it together. I could also see the mayhem in her eyes: the panic, the wrecking ball of grief swinging again. She scrambled to find another cigarette and light it, taking a few furious hits before looking at me. Her big eyes were swollen up with tears. I felt terrible, silently cursing myself, but in my mind, it was important to have this out in the open. Her lips trembled as she attempted to speak. It took her a couple of tries before she managed to reply.

"I understand, Mr Storm, I so understand..."

TWO

I LEFT MY OFFICE AN hour later, a little shell-shocked; the experience had been draining and I felt emotionally deflated. I don't do emotional – not in anything work related anyway. Professional detachment was my natural mode of working. It was the only way to keep myself on an even keel. I didn't want to take home the detritus I dealt with at work. And it was crucial that I kept a calm, cold view on everything whilst working. I couldn't let myself be blinded by feelings. That's how catastrophic mistakes were made. Call me a cynic, but I'm a fixer, not a charity worker. However, Ariella's grief was intense and her demand for my services was even more so. That was something I'd been annoyed about at the time, but fair enough. Broken and lost she might be, but now she had a focus again and that had given her some much-required strength.

I locked the main office door behind me, having sent Petite home twenty minutes earlier. It was early Friday evening, and the city of Edinburgh was gearing up towards yet another party night. The festival was over, but Edinburgh never slept - the greatest little city in the world. I looked up at the steel-grey sky and pulled the collar up on my black leather coat. Apart from the weather, that was. Another miserable evening coming up, of a character only Scotland could really produce. Rain showers, a biting wind and bone-freezing cold, all coming together to test the determination of those venturing out tonight.

I stood for a moment on the grand stone staircase of the building where my office was, and filled my lungs with fresh air. My brother and I had jointly inherited the building from our parents, who'd both been killed in a car crash. I was sixteen and in a private boarding school at the time, whilst my older brother had just completed his probation period with Lothian and Borders Police. We both fell off the rails after that. My grades went south but the Army accepted me nonetheless, whilst my brother managed to keep cool enough to perform in the police. But we offloaded the building as fast as we could; it was worth a cool million. I had the foresight to keep a first-floor flat, which I later converted to my office. But my brother took all his share of the money, and boy did he party! He spent like a lunatic, with me coming a decent second. Grief is a funny thing, it comes in many guises.

My mobile buzzed in my pocket; I fished it out and noticed that I'd received several calls from different numbers, but the one currently calling was Helena, my wife. I swiped the screen and answered.

"Hello darling, I'm on my way. That last meeting took longer than I anticipated." I started walking down the stairs as I said that. It was time to head home.

"Okay my love, can you stop and get some milk on your way?" Helena's voice was very distinctive. She had a generic English accent, pure and clear, evidence of a childhood spent in a succession of private schools abroad, as the family had followed her father's international business career.

"Sure, anything else – wine?" I suggested with a smile. Helena always put me in a good mood. To me, her vibe was pure, positive energy. Her crystal-clear laughter washed away the last of the dread that had attached itself to me from my last client.

"No need Hugo, got plenty!"

"Right then darling, see you soon. Love you!"

I had arrived at my car, an Audi S8, a huge executive saloon with four-wheel drive and a bonkers 5.2 V8 up front! A stonking 450 bhp sat restlessly in the engine bay, just begging me to lose my licence. I'd been very close a few times but so far, so good, I only had six points. I loved the massive sledge even though the car cost a fortune to run and maintain. Over-engineered, so if something were to go wrong, I'd been warned that the bills would be fantastically expensive. So far, my car hadn't needed any of that, but I would need new tyres all round soon, and that already threatened my sound night's sleep.

Another buzz from my mobile. I checked the screen again as I snuggled myself into the plush, leather driver's seat. It was a text from Emily, my eldest: twelve years of age and my special princess. She lived with my ex-wife but even so we had a close and true relationship. That was crucial to me. Moving out and away from Emily had been just about the hardest thing I'd ever done. Claire, her mother, didn't want to be with me any more after I was sentenced to an 18-month stint in Edinburgh Central Prison for beating to a pulp my then-boss in the SIFIS (Serious Insurance Fraud Investigation Services). The guy was a dangerous sexual predator of young vulnerable women, so I never lost any sleep over what I'd done. But I lost Claire and almost lost Emily too; that I did lose sleep over. After release from prison I worked hard to keep up my contact with Emily and we were close once more. My parents were no longer around – through no fault of their own – but, even when they were alive, my brother and I were only a small part of their lives. I'd sworn to myself that I wasn't going to be that kind of a dad to my children.

As soon as I got out of prison I started my current business. With a criminal record, nobody was going to employ me, so Storm Consulting was born. It was just right for me. I never did well in large organisations anyway. Too much of a loner. Too much of a rebel. As Major Brown, from my British Army Intelligence Unit days, had said with a wry smile: "We've got to let you go, Sergeant Storm. You're a brilliant bloke but you've got authority issues!" Summed it up really.

I fired up the beast up front, and fired off a quick text reply to Emily, where I promised to call her later. Before I slotted the gear lever into drive I checked the other missed calls and saw my brother had called a couple of times, as well as a withheld number. There were three messages waiting on the voice mail. I debated with myself whether I wanted to listen to any of those messages there and then; I'd already spoken to my wife, and texted Emily. My other three kids were too young to be phoning me, so there really wasn't anybody else I wanted to speak to at that time. It was Friday evening and I was off. I'd arranged to go to Mrs Cantor's residence tomorrow to commence the case. Rich people live in residences you understand, not homes. Anyway, tomorrow I would also get my retainer, which was badly needed.

Mrs Cantor had money, serious money and so hadn't even flinched when I quoted her my fee. On the spot I had decided to increase my rates and had yanked them up twofold. As a sweetener I told her that, for the added premium, I'd focus only on her case. She didn't hesitate and signed the papers immediately; her only caveat was that I should start the very next day. As I already had plans for the weekend I hesitated, but not for long, as the money spoke and, as per usual, I listened. Remembering this made me think about the forthcoming case. It was like searching for the proverbial needle in a haystack. As far I as I could remember there weren't any strong leads on this case. Chloe had simply vanished, fate unknown. I knew there was a lot to Ariella Cantor that I would need to investigate; she had an interesting background. The police task force had tapped into some of it, but I suspected there was much more to this than had been reported in the media.

Whilst driving home, my mobile rang again. Thinking it could be Helena I answered with the hands-free. Bruce Springsteen's 'Murder Incorporated', which had been blasting out through the car's surround-sound music system, went mute as my brother's angry voice filled the void.

"Why the blazes aren't you answering my calls, Hugo!" he roared. I could hear music and noise in the background and assumed he was out in a bar somewhere.

"Steady Douglas, I'm answering now! Anyway, I'm on my way home – what do you want?" My annoyance was clear from my tone. It'd be fair to say that he and I had a complicated relationship; sometimes we were close and good friends, other times we were feuding furiously and wouldn't see each other for months at a time. Just now we were having a good period and seeing each other regularly. Judging by his tone though, that seemed to be coming to an abrupt end! My brother was seven years older than me and was a Detective Sergeant in the Specialist Crime Division of Police Scotland. He was currently working as an integrated employee with The National Crime Agency, which is a UK-based national law-enforcement agency, on a two-year secondment. I wasn't quite sure what he was actually working on as he'd been pretty secretive about it all. He wouldn't give me any details. I assumed it was a UK-wide organised-crime operation, involving some serious drug trafficking. True to say, Douglas Storm was a legend in Scottish law-enforcement circles, and in more ways than one, both for the good and the bad. The man was controversial and bordering on being a rogue operator; on more than one occasion Internal Affairs had looked into his practices, but so far they hadn't managed to get anything to stick. There was no denying it, Douglas got results. My instinct told me there were parts of Douglas' life I really didn't want to know about.

"I need to see you, Hugo – now!" It was more of a command than a request, and that really got my back up.

"I don't like your tone, Douglas. I'm on my way home. Helena's expecting me," I replied as I steered my car through the early-evening traffic.

"Come on Hugo, I need to see you – wouldn't ask if it wasn't important." Douglas spoke in a forced-friendly manner. He was thick skinned and didn't really care that I was annoyed.

"Yeah well, not tonight brother. Why don't you tell me now?" I braked as the traffic came to a standstill.

"Can't, not over the phone. Never mind. I'll get back to you!" There was a pause and then Douglas terminated the call.

Suit yourself Douglas, I thought to myself as I cursed the heavy traffic. There appeared to be roadworks ahead. There were always roadworks going on in Edinburgh. I'd been too busy talking to Douglas to notice the diversion sign earlier.

Helena and I lived in a nice detached house in Colinton with our three young children: two-year-old twins, Ella and Ryan, and James, who's four, together with Alfie, the Bernese Mountain Dog. It was a busy household in a nice neighbourhood. Not the biggest in the estate but big enough for us. Emily had her own bedroom in the house; that was important to me. She was the big sister and very much part of our family. Although she didn't live with us and sometimes didn't even visit us for weeks on end, Helena knew better than to ever suggest that Emily's room be used for anything else; I wouldn't stand for that. I swung into the driveway an hour late, my mobile ringing again as I was getting out of the car. Part of my life that damned thing, and it rang just about constantly. With a shopping bag in one hand and my leather man-bag swung over my shoulder, I answered before checking the caller id.

"Yes, Hugo Storm here." I answered sternly; I was off duty.

"Hugo Storm, this is Mike Law, one of Mr Bullard's associates." The voice was light but at the same time threatening. It stopped me in my tracks.

"Yes, I spoke to Mr Bullard earlier on. What do you want?" I replied angrily. I knew perfectly well what he wanted but I didn't want to deal with it right then.

"Right mate, you spoke to Mr Bullard earlier, but Mr Bullard was not happy with the outcome of that conversation; it wasn't at all satisfactory to our needs."

Mr Law spoke with a London accent. I knew this guy – he was one of Mr Bullard's main muscle-guys but one with a brain too – a brutal and ruthless operator that worked as the outfit's senior enforcer. I stood in the driveway, thinking hard. This guy was on to me now, and I knew I had to deal with this sooner rather than later. But I wasn't one of their helpless victims who they could just push around. The guy needed to be told that.

"Listen Mike – we're not mates – and I don't deal with minions like you – regardless of how big your ego is! Tell Mr Bullard I'm sorting the money situation and will get back to him on Monday. Tell Mr Bullard I will sort this out to his full satisfaction, and that will be done sooner rather than later. You got that?" I snarled sternly.

There was a pause on the other end as I could hear his breathing hiking up a notch. The guy was angry; he didn't like the way I'd spoken to him but that was just tough.

"Hugo Storm, don't be an idiot! You think you're something big, eh? Listen mate, you owe us money! A lot of money and we want it now. Just exactly who do you think you are?"

The niceties had gone now. I could practically feel the anger venting through my mobile.

"Shut up! Tell Mr Bullard what I told you, and don't you ever dare call me again! Understand?"

I terminated the call and stood for a moment looking at the screen, waiting for the gangster to call again but he didn't. I cursed inwardly as I walked up to the front door, this was something I could've done without. Maybe I'd have to dig into the cash reserve I'd stashed away in my house safe. Not having money and really not having money were two different things. My job incurred a lot of expenses and I needed to be cash loaded at all times. Certain things were only fixed by envelopes under the table. Without that option, I was out of business. Now though, I was heading towards using that money just to stay afloat. Just as I was about to curse loudly, the front door swung open and Helena stepped out. I could see the worry in her face and I knew she'd seen, and possibly heard, me from the kitchen window.

"Everything okay, lover?" she asked, studying my face, "Who called you?"

She paused and looked at the street behind us. Helena had learned to cope with my unorthodox employment and the elements of risk that it entailed.

"Yes, everything's fine, it was just a grumpy individual whose part of something I'm working on just now!"

I lied with a straight face and waited for Helena's judgement. Sometimes I knew she didn't really believe what I told her, but to her credit she took it all as an adult. Early on I'd told her that for her own sanity and safety I couldn't involve her in what I was doing. I needed to stay sharp in my chosen profession and that often meant keeping things to myself. That also kept me on the edge, sharp and finely tuned, so to speak. Anyway, sharing the details of what I did would only seed rot in our relationship; I believed that sincerely. Obviously, in this particular case, I was lying out of self-interest, but that couldn't be helped either. Helena looked at me intensely and I could sense that she was considering whether to continue pushing on with this or whether to back off. She chose to back off, and stepped forward to give me a hug.

"Just tell me one thing, Hugo – are you or we in any danger?" she whispered in my ear.

"Listen, I am, and more importantly, we are safe. I'm a big boy and I'll take care of this!"

I grabbed her tighter, but I could tell that she knew I was lying. But she was a big girl, so she let it slide, relaxing in my arms for a while before pushing herself free.

"Right then, Hugo. Dinner's ready. Love you!"

She smiled and turned to go back in the house. I gazed upon her curved figure as she stepped back inside, and felt a surge of excitement. My wife just turned me on, even dressed in casual clothing and without any make up. How come she loved somebody like me? I silently asked myself this, for the umpteenth time as I followed her into our home. She was a bigger person than me and I was an incredibly lucky guy.

THREE

ARIELLA CANTOR LIVED in a proper Grand Designs house that the guy on the TV would've waxed lyrical about: a stylish detached house, funky even, with a manicured garden and some serious, though discreet, security measures in place. I was sitting in her grand sitting room, taking in the various works of art on the walls and the delicate interior design. How a kid lived here baffled me somewhat, but each to their own. I guessed Chloe had, early on, developed a sense of restraint when it came to jumping around in the house. My kids would've, without a doubt, caused mayhem within an hour of being here.

A man in his late fifties, smartly dressed in an expensive suit, was dominating the floor and voicing his disappointment with our agreement. That man was Aaron David Cantor, and he had made a point of using all three names! The epitome of pomp and arrogance, I decided, after about ten seconds of meeting him. But he was also a serious player, tall and well built, ticking every box on the alpha-male check list. He was Ariella's brother-in-law and, by the looks of him, appeared to be taking ownership of this situation. I glanced over at Ariella and saw that she was looking at him with annoyance as he repeatedly voiced his doubts about me and what he regarded as my outlandish fee. This wasn't my house, so I didn't intervene, but I also had a limit and that was fast approaching.

"I have heard things about you, Mr Storm, and I am none too happy. Granted, my firm have used you in the past and my partners have nothing but praise for your capabilities, but I am not sure that you can add any value here, other than to yourself, by draining my sister-in-law's bank account!"

He'd stopped pacing and had squared himself up in front of me. I looked at him again. 'Add value?' Well, he was speaking true to form, as a banker! But he was way out of order. It was time to lay down the law. I looked over at Ariella and caught her attention.

"Mrs Cantor, I work for you, not your brother-in-law. If he is to be involved, then I'm afraid we've got to end this here and now."

I paused and kept my eyes on Ariella, ignoring the man in front of me. He didn't like that and was about to say something else when Ariella raised her hand and shut him down. I was impressed; I guessed not many people – if any – had ever shut this guy down before. We both looked at her. I studied her expression closely; this lady carried authority. Having commanded our attention, Ariella spoke with a strong voice.

"Oh, shut up David! Listen, Chloe is my daughter and I make the decisions here. I want Mr Storm and that's final." She paused and looked directly at me. Some strength had returned to her demeanour.

"Ariella – what are you thinking?"David questioned her in a condescending tone.

Arrogance epitomised, I thought. I looked at him and decided that if I were to continue with this case, I would first have to take a good long look at Mr Aaron David Cantor. I also instinctively knew that this guy had realised that, and something told me he didn't like it.

"I will do anything to get Chloe back, David, and so I need Mr Storm. Nobody else has delivered, and that includes that useless private detective firm you got on the case. How much have they charged, by the way?"

With that she took a small sip from the glass tumbler of whisky. The ice cubes clinked as she put it down. The lady had excellent taste in beverages. She'd offered me a glass of the high quality single malt, but I'd declined. I wasn't too keen on alcohol – single malt or not – besides I was driving.

David didn't reply. He just nodded, kept his silence and stood staring at Ariella as she stared back. He was getting very angry though. I could almost feel his fury. She didn't back down though, and an ominous silence descended upon the room as a brief but intense power struggle ensued. I wondered what their relationship was truly like; it was obvious that there was a lot of tension between them – I'd noticed it as soon as I was invited in. I had no doubt that he could override her if he so desired, but there was something holding him back. I couldn't figure it out. They continued to glare at each other as I allowed my thoughts to spin.

I was remembering the death of Victor Cantor, Ariella's late husband and Chloe's father, just under five years ago. He'd been found dead, washed up on the beach at South Queensferry, by a dog walker. Somebody had called the local newspaper right after the police were notified and the subsequent media coverage was extensive, with headlines in bold letters. Victor Cantor had been an interesting character to put it mildly: an Edinburgh-based international financier with dealings all over the world – some of them of questionable nature. Amongst other things, the Cantor Finance Group facilitated the trading of international arms, including to and from Israel. The firm had an International Arms Dealer licence issued by the UK Ministry of Defence, but they were a steady target for the investigative journalism of a certain news outlet. Dirt was frequently found but somehow never stuck.

Victor had last been seen leaving his plush office late on the day before he was pulled out of the sea. His Mercedes S-class was discovered, parked and locked, at the south side of the Forth Road Bridge. His expensive Italian-leather shoes were found, placed neatly together, beside the railing, midway along the bridge. It was assumed that he'd climbed and jumped to his death at some point in the early hours of the morning. I remembered noting that, unusually, the CCTV system on the bridge had not been working for about four hours that night. If Victor jumped, he did so without being caught on camera. The speculations were rife, but no hard evidence of sinister acts ever came to light. I remembered the cops I talked to at that time telling me of their suspicions, but nothing of any substance could be found. A few fingers had pointed at David – even I was referring to the man by his middle name now – Victor's brother and business partner, but again nothing solid could be proven. David was determinedly aggressive in his litigation against anybody who dared to suggest that he'd been involved in the death of his brother. And he had very deep pockets, and an army of killer lawyers at his disposal. Even the tabloid newspapers, despite smelling tricks and blood, backed off.

The case was eventually closed, a suicide verdict having been reached, which didn't make much sense to me, but what did I know? As the cops said at the time, it was a true stinker, but there were no solid leads. Ariella hadn't reported her husband missing until just an hour before he was found. The marriage was on the rocks and apparently it wasn't unusual for Victor to not come home for days on end. Items of the family's dirty washing were thoroughly exposed in the media coverage, yet I could tell this had only scratched the surface. This family had more than its fair share of dirty secrets and whole skeletons were hidden in the cupboards, but which of these were rumours and which were facts?

The firm, although based in Edinburgh, did business all around the world, from Tel Aviv to Moscow, London to Islamabad, and beyond. Once again, my old contacts within the Lothian and Borders Police, as well as my brother, provided me with off-the-record information, and I quickly learnt that even the police had difficulty providing a clear picture. The structure of the firm and its dealings was almost insanely complicated. This wasn't new in international arms trading: the more complicated the better, so it seemed. The police activity continued until the MOD moved in and forced them to back off – a shocker to the system, but the top brass had dutifully heard the whisper and had acted promptly. This was not common knowledge; I only heard about it through my contacts. Powerful vested interests were getting annoyed, and had moved to shut down the investigation. Rumour had it that this pressure had actually originated with certain powerful individuals within the Scottish Government.

I had no dealings with this case, but I liked to keep myself informed; Edinburgh was my town. Knowing what the rich, famous and shady were up to was essential in my line of work. Anyway, at that time, I hoped that any measure of insight might benefit me at some point in the future. Now that insight might even be of assistance in the forthcoming hunt for Chloe. Could the Cantor's complicated family business have been a factor in Chloe's disappearance?

"Well Ariella, I think you are being unreasonable here," David broke the silence.

I looked at Ariella and saw the defiance in her face. You go girl, I thought to myself. Standing up to this guy couldn't be easy. Her eyes narrowed and as she leaned forward her fragile slender frame suddenly appeared strong and capable. She was evidently going to give it a go.

"No David, I am not being unreasonable. In fact, I think it's time for you to leave!"

She stood up as she said that, and I looked at David, wondering how he would react. There are several types of alpha male, but only two main categories, in my view. First, the thinking type – those are truly dangerous. Second, the instinct-driven type – those are impulsive and thus less dangerous because they act before they think, and if one kept that in mind, one could manipulate them. I waited with interest to see which of these main categories Ariella's brother would fall into. If it came to it, I was prepared to intervene and throw him out myself, but David simply nodded, showing no resistance. The way he looked at Ariella was weird though. Then he turned, fixed his eyes upon me and smiled ominously.

"Right then Ariella, have it your way! Don't come to me though when this 'gentleman' has bled you dry."

He kept his eyes on me and I saw the veiled threat. This guy wasn't finished by a long shot.

"Leave, David – don't say any more, just leave!"

Ariella's voice was clear and strong. I was surprised again by her authority, and so, apparently, was David. He looked back to her, broke a cold smile and then, without further ado, turned and left. I watched him go, and I knew this guy was dangerous; he dressed like a banker and spoke like a stuck-up snob, but he was pure menace beneath the façade. After he left the house, Ariella glanced at me and I saw the pain return. It was obvious that her show of strength had completely drained her. She sat back in the chair and took a hit of the whisky.

"I am sorry about David, Mr Storm. My brother-in-law is quite bossy and protective; he just can't help it!"

She attempted a smile. Her words didn't ring true to me. However, I left it at that.

"Don't apologise to me, Mrs Cantor. I just need to reiterate one particular caveat of this contract: I work for you and only you! I answer to nobody else," I paused and took a moment to consider how to word my next thought. I decided just to say it, "And you understand that I will look at everything and everybody in my search for Chloe!"

I paused again to allow her to digest what she had heard. Ariella was an intelligent lady; she understood perfectly well the implications of what I had just said. I was going to look at good old David as well as the rest of her family.

After a minute she nodded and replied, "I would expect nothing less, Mr Storm!"

It had not, however, escaped my notice that she had had to think about it for a moment before agreeing. I decided to keep my own counsel on that, at least for the time being.

My mobile vibrated in my pocket. It was on silent, so I ignored it. It was time to get down to business here. I leaned forward and looked directly at Ariella.

"Right, before we continue we need to address the issue of my fee. As we discussed, I need an up-front retainer, paid immediately, and then I'll furnish you with a weekly bill."

I felt the need to address this despite the fact that Ariella's brother-in-law had, just minutes ago, implied that I was nothing but a money-obsessed hustler, whose sole aim was to take as much money off her as possible. Nonetheless, this was business, and I was the real deal; that was why she came to me in the first place. I wasn't a charity worker and thus my services were premium with a premium rate attached. I had huge overheads which needed to be covered – easy as that. Ariella just nodded; this was an individual who wasn't confused by morality and money. She knew I was the business and that was what she wanted.

"That's fine, Mr Storm. How can I facilitate this now?" she asked.

"I can take card payment, or we can arrange a money transfer right now."

I lifted my leather briefcase, which contained a card-paying machine. All that was needed was WIFI. This little machine was state-of-the-art technology, shipped from the US, and designed to streamline my revenues just nicely! If that didn't appeal, she could use her online banking and transfer the money immediately. Either way, I wasn't going to make a move until my retainer had safely landed in my designated bank account.

"I can transfer the money right now, Mr Storm. Would that suit?" Ariella enquired. "Money transfer is fine with me," I replied.

"Good, now let me find my phone and I will call my business manager and she can transfer the money right way."

Ariella stood up and started searching for her phone. I waited and mulled over my thoughts. We'd previously discussed things and agreed on my fee but I hadn't really been specific about my retainer. Yesterday she'd been on the edge; I wasn't sure how much of our conversation she'd remember. I was just wondering how to deal with that when she came back with a mobile, looked at me and broke a sad little smile.

"Ms Kim Monteith is always on call. She speaks five languages and is very smart, you understand. Travels more than I, and has contacts all over the world. Anyway, I am digressing here, let me get this money transferred."

I didn't comment, not my business anyway. Ariella worked the mobile and somebody answered on the other side.

"Kim, can you please drop everything and do something important for me right away?" Ariella leaned against a funky metal bookcase.

I looked at her and saw a very elegant but lonely figure. I assumed Kim complied with the request and Ariella spoke again.

"I need to transfer some money immediately. Use one of the Zurich accounts."

I suppressed a smile. I wasn't the only one with bank accounts abroad, although mine were all running rather low at that time, due to unfavourable circumstances.

"How much for the retainer?" enquired Ariella.

That confirmed it – I hadn't been specific enough. Getting out my leather wallet, I fished out a card for an account I had with a discreet small bank on the Isle of Man. It was the type of bank that didn't advertise, and thus attracted customers who liked that. I walked over to her, handed her the card, and calmly stated: "£15,000".

Ariella didn't even bat an eyelid, but told Kim to transfer £15,000 straight away to the bank account I'd provided, clearly stating the details and waiting for confirmation. Kim was efficient, and within a few minutes the money had been transferred.

"Thank you, Kim. I will see you later in the office." Ariella hung up.

I decided I would check the account myself as soon as I could, but there was no reason to believe that the money hadn't gone in.

"So, Mr Storm what now?" Ariella asked.

"Right, Mrs Cantor, I need to familiar myself with Chloe and the circumstances of her disappearance. What can you tell me?"

I expected her to take me to her case room, so to speak. Most caring parents whose child goes missing will accumulate and keep all available information about their child's case. Some will create advanced filing systems as the search engulfs their lives. Ariella's house was big enough for a designated room.

"Well, Mr Storm, come with me," she replied after a moment.

Ariella got up and walked towards the wood and glass staircase. I followed as she led the way up to the first floor. We entered a room off the large landing and, as I suspected, Ariella had indeed got a case room. It was a large bedroom that'd been cleared of all the usual furniture. It now contained a couple of bookcases, filing cabinets and maps and drawings on a huge cork board, which filled one wall. There was also a table and a couple of chairs situated in the middle of the room. Although there was plenty of light from the two big windows, the atmosphere in the room felt cold and depressive, but then again, it contained the horrors of Chloe's disappearance.

I sat down, looked around and wondered if the specific lead to finding Chloe, dead or alive, was in this room. Or was all this nothing but noise? Ariella sat down on the other side of the table and she too looked around. We both sat in total silence for a while, whilst I assessed the space. The presence of the missing child was very strong in the room. I could feel it.

"I don't know how many hours I've spent looking through all this,"

Ariella spoke quietly and waved a manicured hand around. I waited a moment, before I spoke.

"What do you have in here? Everything from the police, I guess?"

"Yes, I've got copies of everything the police have. My lawyers made sure of that. Also, the reports – useless as they were – from the private investigator firm which David hired, but which I paid for obviously!" Ariella lit another cigarette as she recalled this.

"Who did you use?" I asked curiously.

"BRP Investigation Services. Do you know about them?"

Ariella looked at me enquiringly. I nodded in response, Edinburgh wasn't that big. I knew BRP – decent enough outfit but in my view not up to a job like this.

"Yes, decent private investigators I would say – used here in Edinburgh and Glasgow by the corporate world and private citizens alike," I said and looked back at Ariella. Her green eyes had regained a little light.

"Well, please help yourself to their reports if you like, Mr Storm. They are all there."

She pointed to a deep drawer in a filing cabinet.

"Thank you," I said, and paused before continuing, "I presume I have access to everything in this room – there isn't anything in here that's off limits?"

I waited for a response. Ariella looked around the room as if trying to remember whether there was anything in there that I shouldn't see. Old habits, I decided. She'd lived a secretive life; it was probably deeply ingrained. Satisfied, she shook her head.

"Please, Mr Storm, feel free; nothing is off limits in here. Excuse my curiosity, but how do you intend to work this case?"

It was a valid question that required a proper answer.

"I'll trust my instincts here. The police, and to a much lesser degree those private investigators, have done a lot of the leg work already. There's no point in my walking those miles all over again. What I need to do is to walk the cat back and see if anything pops out,"

"Walk the cat back?" Ariella asked.

"Yes, forgive me, it's an expression used by western spy agencies during the cold war to expose double agents. One would take a case involving a certain agent or agents, start with the end game and work backwards to the start. This approach worked for both general fishing expeditions, as in casting a net wide and seeing what one caught, or for specific hunts when one went after known suspects. With such a methodology, different and often overlooked aspects of a case would appear. This way of working could reveal new information that's already there but was previously unnoticed. Information gathering is a specialised field in which methodology is vital to unlock secrets that are already there."

I paused, allowing the lady time to digest what I'd said.

"I see, I think I understand. How do you know this? And how does this apply here?"

Ariella stubbed out her cigarette in a crystal ashtray on the table.

"I served with British Army Intelligence. I was also a serious fraud investigator for a premium insurance house. I was good at it too, but you know this otherwise you wouldn't have come to me. Anyway, I'll utilise the same principle: start with the latest information available and then chronologically work myself back to the day Chloe went missing. Then I'll look at all the people in both your lives."

"Interesting!" declared Ariella after some quiet thoughtfulness, "Well, I will leave you to it, but before I go, can I get you anything? Coffee? Some food perhaps? My House Assistant will be here soon. Her cooking is delicious, would you like some lunch?"

'House assistant': a euphemism for house maid, I assumed. Ariella suddenly appeared to be in a hurry. I don't know if she needed to escape the room or attend to something else important, but she needed to get out for sure. I guessed that she found this room either impossible to leave, or impossible to be in; one that she couldn't leave quick enough. Grief is a fluid process that seldom makes sense, and is always changing over the course of time; something that may have once been comforting can become the exact opposite. People's behaviour can and will be erratic and hard to understand, but for the most part I was getting Ariella here. Or was I getting just what she wanted me to get? I told myself to stop the conspiracy thinking and get on with it!

"Yes, to both please. Black coffee with one sugar please," I said, and rose to have a stretch. Ariella nodded and attempted a smile again, this time succeeding. She brushed past me; I strongly sensed her womanhood and felt a brief sexual tension that I found disturbing. Pull yourself together man! I thought to myself as she left the room.

The next six hours were spent locked away in my room, trying to absorb as much information about the case as I possibly could. To be able to focus properly I did something I almost never do: I turned my mobile off. Then I went to work. I'm a quick reader and have a sharp mind. Fairly quickly, a mind map of what I was ploughing through established itself in my brain. Ariella kept away, which was just as well as it allowed me to focus. At six o' clock I called it a day. I'd filled a big cardboard box with files that I was going to study at home. Ariella didn't have any problem with that. She'd been working too; I found her at her desk in her office on the other side of the landing. She was so engrossed in her laptop that she didn't notice me to begin with. Maybe this was the only time she could, albeit fleetingly, escape the internal horror she probably battled every single second of her day. I knew Chloe was nailed to her vision throughout the day and surfaced constantly in her ongoing nightmares; she'd told me as much.

"Well, Mrs Cantor, I'll see you tomorrow at nine."

She turned around as I said this. Tomorrow was Sunday, but I was being paid a premium rate here.

"Thank you, Mr Storm, see you tomorrow. Lynne will show you out. Goodbye."

With that, Ariella returned to her laptop, and I went on my way. Lynne was downstairs and hurried to let me out. She was a plump but pleasant older lady who sported, by the looks of it, a permanent smile. I thanked her once more for my delicious lunch and said goodbye. I placed the cardboard box in the boot of my car and, just as I was about to slot myself in behind the wheel, I sensed something, looking up I saw Ariella standing looking at me from the first-floor window. She didn't appear to acknowledge me but stood still, watching me. I nodded and slotted myself into the car. Damn, I felt that chill again.

FOUR

I WAS JUST ABOUT TO drive off when my mobile rang. I'd checked it before getting into the car, and had seen the missed call. Somebody with a withheld number had called but hadn't left any message. That annoyed me as this was a new mobile with a new SIM card, one from my stash, which I kept in my home-office safe. I hadn't circulated this number yet, the only person who knew it so far was Helena. I pushed away the dark thoughts, smiled and answered with a happy tone. I remembered something my brother had once told me – he'd heard it from a police shrink – smiling helps to maintain a happy mind. Of course, my brother had instantly dismissed that as utter garbage, but me – I was still game.

"Sorry for being late darling. On my way home now."

"Hugo, I don't know how to say this ..." Helena's voice was filled with panic.

I froze, suddenly feeling acutely aware of everything around me. Helena was, by nature, as far removed from hysterical as anyone I'd ever known. She simply refused to panic. In fact, she'd survived and even thrived in dicey situations abroad as a young person, when her host countries had erupted in war and violent civil conflicts. Her dad's business had taken the family to some rather dangerous places and, even though Helena's childhood was a world of privilege, that world was sometimes jarringly shattered by a nasty reality exploding right outside her home. But her dad had told me with pride, after a few gin and tonics, that Helena always displayed an incredible sense of calm when the dirt hit the proverbial fan. I'd seen that for myself, first hand. In a pressed and stressed state of mind Helena would be nothing but steady and rational. She'd eventually fall apart, as everybody did, but not until afterwards. So, her now being in what appeared to be a total state of panic just about freaked me out.

"What, Helena, just tell me – what is wrong?"

"Claire called – Emily's missing!"

Helena blurted out these dreadful words and then fell silent. With that, the bottom dropped out of my world.

"What are you saying?" I demanded.

Unable to process what I'd just heard, I felt like I'd been hit by a hammer and the whole world around me went blurry; this couldn't be happening! Keep it together, I told myself. This is about Emily, not you!

"Claire called a couple of minutes ago, hysterical, simply saying Emily was missing ...where are you, Hugo, where are you?"

Helena sobbed as she asked the question. My thoughts were racing. I needed to speak to Claire. Now!

"Listen Darling, I've got to call Claire. Did she say where she was?" There was a growing urgency in my voice.

"At home, as far as I understand. Please keep me updated Hugo. I love you."

"Will do. I love you too. Bye."

I terminated the call and immediately dialled Claire's house, suppressing the panic I felt. My kids were off limits, bad stuff could and would happen to me, but my kids – no!

Calm down. I told myself. It's nothing, I lied to myself. After a few rings a male voice answered. It was Tom, Claire's boyfriend, a guy I'd begrudgingly allowed to become 'step-dad' to Emily. Tom was okay, bland but solid, and somebody Emily had grown to really like – love even – a sore subject for me to have to deal with, but such was life. Now though, all of that didn't matter one iota.

"Tom, its Hugo. Let me speak to Claire!"

"Oh damn! ... Sorry Hugo, I don't know if she... can you hold?"

Tom was obviously very confused. He left the phone just as I started to curse; my emotions were gaining ground on me. This was not going be fine; I just knew it. I flipped the gear lever into drive and slammed my foot down on the accelerator. The big beast jumped forward and an approaching car had to do an emergency stop as I tore into the street. I didn't care. I floored the accelerator. The call was on hands-free anyway. I drove as fast as I could through the leafy streets of Ariella's Edinburgh. I could feel the veins throbbing in my neck.

"Sorry Hugo, Claire can't manage to talk just now. You on your way?"

Tom was back on the line. I could hear other people in the background. What exactly was going on?

"On my way," I said through gritted teeth, and terminated the call.

I focused on the driving, not allowing anything else to distract me. Emily missing! The only thing I knew was that I needed to get to Claire as fast as I possibly could.

Emily, Claire and Tom still lived in the neat two-bedroomed bungalow that Claire and I had bought together all those years ago. A nice home in a nice little street in the Portobello area of Edinburgh. I'd signed the place over to her when I moved out as I didn't want to upset Emily's life more than I had to. Her little family breaking up was enough trauma for a little soul, in my view.

I got there without being stopped by the police, which was lucky considering the way I'd been driving. As I arrived I saw several police cars parked outside and more than the usual number of other cars parked all around the street. I saw a free spot at the kerb close to the bungalow and rammed my Audi in. A couple of uniformed police officers promptly approached me as I jumped out. Both were determined and ready to confront me; I'd entered the street in a hurry.

"Officers, I'm Hugo Storm – Emily's dad!" I announced and marched determinedly past them.

"Oh, understood sir," said the older officer.

I was already past and entered the property, before he could ask anything else. The house was full of people, and a quick tally confirmed that they were mostly Claire's family and friends. Claire had a close family, and they saw each other all the time. Some people looked at me with surprise and several looked away. There were others present who I didn't recognise. Anger swelled up inside, as it dawned on me that I hadn't been the first person Claire had contacted regarding what had happened to our daughter, not by a long shot. But this wasn't the time to split hairs over my position within the hierarchy of Claire and Emily's family. I quelled my anger and walked down the central corridor that led to the living room at the back of the house. Tom looked out from the kitchen and I saw the panic in his face.

"Hugo, what can I say? Sorry mate!" He didn't know what to do with himself.

"Where's Claire?" I demanded, ignoring all the others, who had all gone silent.

"She's in the living room, Hugo."

I didn't bother with pleasantries and quickly strode the final few steps to the living room. It was like I was standing on a cliff edge and the smallest touch would've pushed me over that edge. I flung the door open and entered the room – more people. Everyone fell silent when they saw me. Claire was sitting on the three-seater with her mother on one side and her older sister on the other, all three were crying. I felt a punch, more like a brutal kick in the back really, and then it felt like I was falling. But I kept standing – holding it together – using my anger to combat the rising panic.

"What in heaven's name is going on, and where's Emily?" My voice, although full of rage, was starting to crack under the emotional strain.

Claire, her mother and her sister looked up at me and I saw the pain in their tear-filled eyes. I felt dizzy, the room seemed to be spinning! I had to focus really hard to remain upright. Somebody laid a hand on my shoulder, and I spun around, my fist clenched, ready to throw a punch.

"Mr Storm, don't! I'm Detective Constable Fuller. Please have a seat!"

"Leave me alone!" I growled, "Somebody had better tell me what on earth is going on here and where my daughter is!"

I was furious and now in a state of panic. I needed answers.

"Somebody took Emily a couple of hours ago, Hugo."

Claire's words made everything stop spinning. I looked back at her and fixed her in my stare.

"What are you talking about, Claire?"

I still couldn't take it in, and my words came out as little more than a strangled whisper.

"There's a witness who says that a little girl fitting Emily's description was bundled into a van a couple of hours ago."

Claire's voice too was barely audible, but I heard it very well. Then she started to cry, burying her head in her mother's comforting bosom.

"That's crazy!" I exclaimed.

My voice was suddenly back with full force. Claire looked back up in response to my loud exclamation.

This was Edinburgh, Scotland, and just another normal Saturday. Here, little girls weren't grabbed off random streets and bundled into random vans. Not here, not my little girl! Claire tried to reply but broke down and started to sob again. I looked at her but felt only numbness. The officer at my side laid his hand on my shoulder again. This time, I felt no aggression. In fact, at that precise moment, I felt just like a deflated balloon. But still I wanted that damned hand off my shoulder.

"Remove your hand," I said in as flat and steady tone of voice as I could muster.

"Mr Hugo Storm, please come with me."

He pointed beyond his left shoulder and I saw another police detective sitting in the chair that used to be my old favourite. Claire had a lot of family but not a lot of money. Even with Tom in the picture I helped out every month. That was cool, it was for Emily anyway.

I took a couple of steps over and scrutinised the detective sitting in the chair. An older guy. I looked hard at him and he looked back at me through weary eyes. I knew who he was, but I couldn't place him right then. My brain had now entered the stage of being fried. But I told myself to get a grip and try to evaluate what was going on here. My Emily was missing. The dizziness became overwhelming again, and I sat myself on a chair opposite the senior plain-clothed police officer.

"Mr Hugo Storm, I am Detective Inspector Angus McGregor from Police Scotland."

He leaned forward, extending a hand as he said that. I shook his hand and then I recognised him. Gus McGregor, the legendary homicide police detective. His nickname in the force was 'The last natural detective in Scotland.' That mattered because he only took on the big cases, and now he was here. My head reeled – what had happened to my little girl?

"Please tell me what's going on here, Inspector?" I implored.

I focused only on him; all the others in the room faded away. He looked at his wristwatch and then opened his police notepad, took a moment and then looked me straight in the eye.

"Right, Emily was last seen leaving her piano teacher's house at 14:11 today, walking down Grant Avenue. Then we have a statement from a witness, who said that Emily was seen getting into a blue transit panel van at 14:14, two blocks from Mr Kemo's house, the piano teacher, also on Grant Avenue. Claire reported Emily missing at 15:06, and we obtained the report of a child possibly being lured into a van at 16:17. Police Scotland declared a major crime incident at 16:18. Since then we've flooded the area with police officers and all resources are at my disposal as we speak."

Detective Inspector McGregor paused to look at me, his face completely neutral, his eyes giving nothing away. I realised that he was studying me, gauging my reaction. I looked at my wristwatch; it read 18:52. My daughter had been missing for more than four hours and I'd only just found out about it.

"This is outrageous! Why did nobody contact me?" I shouted, barely holding it together.

I was so angry with Claire that I felt like going ballistic, but I knew I couldn't. I didn't look in her direction, although I knew she'd heard me, as had everybody else in the room. The Detective Inspector slowly shook his head.

"My apologies, Mr Storm, I can't answer for Ms Munro, but the officer responsible for contacting you got your mobile number wrong and left a message on that number. When we rang your house we got your answering machine. The same with your office number: answering machine. Again, I'm truly sorry for this mistake."

I shook my head and raised a hand in a gesture of 'don't bother'. D.I. McGregor was big enough to accept my anger and remained silent as I tried to get my head around this. Leave it, I told myself, what was important now was finding Emily.

"How certain is this witness that it was really Emily getting into that van?"

I was forcing myself to keep focused and not allowing room for self-pity and anger, which would not help Emily in any way.

"The witness is at the Division HQ, being interviewed by experienced officers. And, judging by his description, it seems likely that it was Emily entering that panel van."

"He didn't intervene – no?" I replied aggressively.

The numbness had gone for now. A hot glowing lump was forming in my stomach. I felt nauseous and dizzy, but I held it together.

"No, as he was unsure what was going on. It could've been a legitimate pick up. It appears that Emily entered the van voluntarily."

So, it hadn't happened the way Claire had said; Emily wasn't bundled into this van. Maybe she was lured in? People's perceptions of the same event can be very different. I knew that well enough from my line of work. I glanced over at Claire who was sitting looking at me, tears streaming down her face. Seeing my anger, she lowered her eyes. I felt a twinge of sympathy as I just knew she would punish herself until Emily was safely returned. If that didn't happen, then she would continue to torment herself until the day she died. And so would I. Claire was a good mother and, despite our differences, she'd never used Emily in any of our battles. I had acted the same. I brought my focus back – here and now – that was what mattered! Blame and guilt could be for a later date; either wouldn't help Emily now, for sure.

"And you don't have the van yet?"

I knew the answer already. My pulse kept racing on, I could feel it in my head. I was more scared than I ever had been. My little girl taken – just about the worst nightmare of any parent.

"No, I'm afraid not. We're actively searching though, and every available unit is out, scouring the region. Police Scotland is ready to go Scotland-wide and every appropriate unit is on high alert. Airports and train stations have also been alerted."

The DI briefly glanced over at his younger colleagues after giving me this reassurance.

"What about Mr Kemo, the piano teacher, you guys talking to him too?"

"Yes, he too is down at HQ, being interviewed by experienced officers," Angus replied.

As he stood up I saw that he was a big man, taller and wider than me, with an impressive bulk going south; the stomach had started to strain on the trousers. Still, D.I. Angus McGregor cut an authoritative figure.

"Listen, Mr Storm, I need you to come with me."

He gave me a strange, melancholy look, which made the hair on the back of my neck stand up on end.

"Why?" I challenged, although I knew exactly why.

The rage inside me stoked up even hotter. But this one little guy in the back of my mind, was telling me to calm it down. Don't dig yourself a grave here!

"You know why. Come on now Hugo, just come with me," he urged in a calm and commanding voice as he stepped forward into my personal space and pointed at the door.

"Where are you taking Hugo? What's going on?"

Claire's panicky voice cut through the tension between me and the Inspector. He raised his left arm in a gesture of 'calm it down'.

"We need to talk to Hugo at the station, Ms Munro."

D.I. McGregor answered her without taking his eyes off me for a moment.

"Why – why – are you taking Hugo away?" she asked again and began to cry.

Angus let out a sigh, looked over at the female officer and nodded. The officer nodded back, gesture understood, and squeezed herself in between Claire and her sister.

"Nothing to worry about, Ms Munro. Detective Inspector McGregor just needs to speak to Mr Storm in private. But we'll keep you fully updated. We must focus on Emily, yes?"

The female officer laid a comforting hand on Claire's shoulder, which was moving up and down in rhythm with her sobs. Claire was completely lost in her own grief for now, and didn't notice my concerned look. Her mother, however, had noticed me, and was staring directly at me. I didn't like her attention! Our relationship had been very rocky at the best of times, and nowadays I didn't have much to do with her at all. She was glaring at me with a judgemental look in her eyes. I was about to say something to her when Angus' meaty hand landed heavily on my shoulder.

"Come on, son. Standing here is a waste of time. Agree?"

His words were gentle but firm as he turned me around. I let him. The other officer looked at me with cold, hard eyes and then led us out. We walked out of the house in silence, and I felt everyone staring at me. Outside we walked up to an unmarked Volvo S60, which was parked in the street, engine running and ready to go with an officer behind the wheel. Angus ushered me into the back seat, sat himself next to me, and a third officer got into the front passenger seat.

FIVE

"YOU DON'T THINK I'VE got anything to do with the kidnapping of my own daughter, Detective Inspector McGregor?"

The words hissed out through clenched teeth. My anger was about to explode but I knew I had to keep it under control. The police were just doing their job, and investigating the family was part of it. That included me, even though I didn't like it. My Emily was missing, and I wanted to get out there looking for her. I needed to cooperate and make sure the Inspector detained me for no longer than was absolutely necessary.

"We don't think anything at the moment, Mr Storm, but we need to establish where you were at the time of the incident."

Detective Inspector McGregor spoke with a relaxed voice; he'd done this many times. Most family tragedies involving missing kids, abuse and other heinous acts turned out to have been perpetrated by family members or close friends. I assumed that on many occasions, McGregor had smooth talked the perpetrator, the very one who, behind the façade of grief, had committed the act in the first place. Just because I came across as a dad in shock didn't necessarily mean that much. And he had a point, I'd been unreachable for several hours, which could be interpreted in various ways. A thought struck me. I glanced over at McGregor. He was deep in thought, but he noticed my changed expression.

"What mobile number did you guys call?" I asked.

He looked back at me, before he focused on the officer in the front seat of the police car.

"Officer Fuller, do we have the number to hand?"

He waited whilst the officer retrieved his police notepad and read out the number. Yes, it was the wrong one.

"That's my old phone, it's at home. I got a new phone yesterday, only started using it today. You left a message on my old phone. This is my new phone,"

I got it out from inside my leather jacket and showed it to Inspector McGregor.

"We called the number Claire Munro gave us, and checked it with the mobile number registered in your business directory," McGregor replied.

"Yes, it is my number – my old one – I've got several phones. I texted this new number to Emily last night telling her to give it to her mum. Hadn't got around to telling Claire myself or updating my business details. The old phone's in the house."

I felt a little better, having explained this to him. The last thing I wanted was to have to sit in McGregor's office whilst he cross-checked everything. I wanted to hit the streets and look for Emily. Where to look I didn't know, but sitting in McGregor's office wouldn't accomplish anything. I felt his intense stare and I stared back; the sleepy eyes of the Detective Inspector were deceptive and didn't give anything away. Did he believe me? His eyes softened a little.

"Right, can you tell me where you've been today?" McGregor asked.

"I started a new case today, and I've been at my client's residence all day."

In my line of work, I often touch base with the police and that wasn't always a happy touch. As a private investigator and trouble-shooter, I often, officially at least, venture close to the line of legality; unofficially, I cross that line all the time. The relationship I had with the police was variable. I had a good one with some of them, probably helped by the envelopes of money which changed hands under the table at times. With others the relationship was toxic. The top brass of Police Scotland, with a few exceptions, considered me a rogue operator and a nuisance. I hadn't dealt with McGregor before and was unsure which camp he belonged to. He arched an eye and I knew he wanted more.

"Can you expand on that, Mr Storm?"

I didn't want to expand on that, but here he was testing me. If he thought I was holding back, then his incentive to help me would be comprised. If he knew that I was genuine and what I wanted more than anything was to get out there and search for my daughter, he might cut me some slack. I decided to lay my cards on the table.

"I've accepted an assignment from Mrs Ariella Cantor to search for her missing daughter, Chloe!"

I paused after blurting this out. McGregor's eyes narrowed whilst he digested this new information.

"You're aware that this is still an active investigation?"

"Yes, Mrs Cantor approached me, and I agreed to look into her case as a private investigator. She has the legal right to do that, it's her child that's missing!"

I stopped abruptly as I suddenly felt like I was going to vomit. The nausea was swirling in my stomach. What had happened had suddenly came back to me with a vengeance. I looked down and fought to regain control. Come on! I told myself.

"Take it easy there, Mr Storm. Yes, she has the right to employ a private investigator. You wouldn't mind if we contacted her though, to verify this?"

McGregor looked around the back of the vehicle, realising the cause of my distress. Not finding what he was looking for, he spoke to the officer in the front seat.

"Fuller, do you have a vomit bag available?"

Fuller frantically searched but couldn't find one.

"Sorry Inspector, but there doesn't seem to be one."

Then Fuller glanced over at the police driver, who ignored this and silently focused even harder on his driving. As in every organisation, the blame went down until it could go no further.

"Okay Fuller, something to consider for the future,"

McGregor's reply was addressed to only Fuller, but it was most definitely aimed at both officers in the front. They nodded and replied in unison. "Yes Sir!"

McGregor knew well the signs that a person that was about to vomit, so he lowered his window. A gust of fresh Edinburgh air reduced the tense atmosphere in the car. I sat back, holding myself together and focused on breathing. I didn't know if my behaviour had made McGregor more sympathetic to my situation or not. I didn't care. I wasn't playing a game here. Composure regained for the moment, I looked back over at him.

"No problem, I'll give you her contact details, and you can speak to her as you wish."

"Good, we'll be at the station soon and then we can get this over and done with," McGregor said as he looked out of his window.

"Okay."

Although I wasn't quite sure what he meant, my brain was a little numb, so I confined my reply to that single word. I nodded, more to myself than to him. Outside, the City of Edinburgh was going on with its business, its people getting on with their busy lives. Emily's disappearance hadn't hit the media yet, but when it did I knew it'd be headline news, and people would take notice, even if only for a fleeting moment. But I knew her case would ultimately be nothing but a footnote in the life of Scotland's capital city. It wasn't the biggest city in the world, but it was my city and I loved it – well, until now I had! Now it was the city that'd taken my oldest daughter. I thought about Emily and her energetic busy personality. She was a joyful child, content and confident, that just brought happiness to everywhere she went. And she was innocent. But all that hadn't helped; she'd still been taken. I felt the nausea again and this time I couldn't stop it. Bending forward I vomited between my legs into the foot well.

"Shit." McGregor reacted in an annoyed tone, "Damn. All right, we'll soon be at the station!" he continued, a little more sympathetically.

McGregor tried to get his large frame as far away from me as possible. I didn't care, my world was falling apart. The car windows came down again and the driver stepped on the gas whilst cursing me. The sour smell of my vomit filled the car, even with the windows down. We came to an abrupt halt outside Police Edinburgh Divisional HQ and McGregor and his colleagues leapt swiftly out of the car. McGregor came around and opened my door. I looked at him apologetically.

"Sorry, couldn't help it."

"Don't worry, I understand. I'll get the car cleaned up. You okay to come with me? Do you need to clean up?"

There was a neutral expression on his face. The police driver said something to McGregor's colleague and they both stifled a laugh. I guessed it wasn't the first time people he'd brought in had vomited in his car, guilty or not, of the heinous crime in question. I checked myself out and realised I'd somehow avoided my clothes, and was clean.

"I'm fine thanks."

I stepped out from the back of the police car just as my mobile rang. McGregor's steely stare scrutinised me as I fished my phone out from my leather jacket. I looked at the screen and saw it was Helena.

"It's my wife, do you mind?" I asked, I didn't know why I felt compelled to ask for his permission, but I just felt weak and rudderless at that moment.

"No, go ahead. I'll see you in my office."

He had quickly considered my request and obviously decided I was too weak to run away. So, granting my request he turned to walk to the front door. I nodded a thank you and swiped the screen to answer. A thought hit me as I heard my wife's anxious voice.

"Helena, just a minute."

I took a few steps to steady myself. I didn't need to do that, but I wanted McGregor and his colleagues out of ear shot before I spoke to her. I could see the junior police officer looking at the inspector with a troubled, questioning face as they walked away. He was waved down and summoned to follow. Once they were far enough away I returned my attention to the mobile.

"Hugo, I'm sick with worry here. What's going on?" Helena's voice was insistent.

"I'm at the Fettes Police HQ, Helena – it's bad – Emily's been abducted!"

I steeled myself. I needed to stay strong now, enough weakness, I could crash later.

"What are you saying, Hugo? I don't understand,"

Helena started to cry. I knew she'd been pacing around, knowing something was terribly wrong. Now she had the confirmation she didn't want. I searched for words before answering.

"Helena, I can't believe it myself. But today somebody snatched Emily up from the street and took her away!"

I paused. Officer Fuller, McGregor's colleague, had emerged from the front door and was standing looking at me. He couldn't hear what I was saying but I felt his stare. He wanted me to come over, now.

"This is unbelievable, Hugo. I can't believe it! Are you absolutely sure?"

Helena's voice was almost breaking as she was forcing the words out. Her cry made my nerves go raw and I had to hold the mobile away from my ear for a moment. The Fuller guy was now beckoning, but there was something I needed to tell Helena first.

"Listen, Helena. This is important. Just do what I say, okay? Get the kids, take one of the new mobiles, put some clothes together, cash from the hidden safe and get in the Discovery. Just leave right now. Go somewhere random, somewhere we haven't been before. Make sure you aren't followed. Call Petite from that mobile only, okay? You listening? I need you to do this."

My instructions were urgent, and my tone conveyed that unequivocally.

"What, this is crazy!"

Helena was an intelligent, capable woman and she understood the ramifications of what I was telling her to do.

"Just do it, and do it now. I don't know what on earth is going on here, but I need you guys to be safe and I don't trust anybody, bar Petite, right now. Please, tell me you're going to do what I just said."

There was a brief pause, which felt like an eternity, before Helena replied.

"Right, I'll get the kids, and leave. Then I'll contact Petite. I love you, Hugo!"

There was determination in her voice. That's my girl, I thought to myself as I terminated the call and quickly worked the menu to call Petite. She'd better flaming answer, I thought to myself as it rang. I gestured to the police officer indicating that I was coming. He was getting impatient.

"Okay, Hugo?" Petite replied through a wall of thumping rave music. She was out somewhere, but her voice was clear and sharp as always, Petite didn't drink. Petite was just too busy consuming life to consider numbing any of her senses.

"Listen, I need you to get ready to meet up with Helena. She and the kids are on the move, and need to get to a safe location, which must remain unknown to everybody. Helena will call you soon. Got it?"

Those were my final, hurried instructions as I started to walk towards a frustrated police officer.

"Got it, Hugo!" Petite answered without delay.

My voice told her not to hesitate and not to ask questions – she knew those questions would be answered later. She was a super-efficient operator, that young lady: sharp, strong and although unconventional in pretty much every aspect of her life, her choices never complicated her work performance. And I trusted her.

"Right then, Mr Storm, follow me, Detective Inspector Mc-Gregor is waiting."

Detective Constable Fuller was clearly irritated by my delay. I gave him a hard look and he immediately busied himself with leading the way. That suited me well. Had he not been a DC, and this not a police station, I would've slapped his self-important face. Instead, I walked with him to Inspector McGregor's office, in silence.

My brain was working at full speed now. Was Emily's kidnapping aimed at me? Heaven knows, I had more than my fair share of enemies, and that included some pretty nasty people in the criminal underworld. Edinburgh, with its stunning cityscape and many unique features, attracted a lot of international tourists, but it's dark underbelly was just as vibrant too. True, Glasgow was bigger, and had a formidable bare-knuckle, gang-land reputation, but Edinburgh could be just as ruthless, if not more so. I'd done many jobs where I'd stepped on the toes of powerful people, and my secret files bulged with sensitive information on the high and mighty of the underworld. Knowledge was power – personal intimate knowledge even more so. There are few things powerful and wealthy people care more about than their reputations and freedom. I had stuff in hidden files that could threaten both of those. Most people suspected I had such files, but nobody had managed to locate them, so far. I wasn't so stupid as to keep them either at home or in the office. Those files were kept in a secure hidden location with digital backups in other secret closed-circuit locations. The optimum cyber security was staying off grid – off line – no hackers could get to that stuff because it simply wasn't reachable online. A simple method I was stunned others didn't use. I was now asking myself whether somebody was hitting me where I was most vulnerable – by hitting my kid? If so, what did he, she or they want from me? Revenge? Information?

SIX

"SIT DOWN MR STORM. Fancy a tea or a coffee?"

The voice of Detective Inspector McGregor brought me back to the present as we both entered his office. I declined, so the Inspector wasted no time and began his formal questioning. I had nothing to hide so I answered truthfully. Initially, his manner was relaxed, but pretty soon he started to prod me on my business dealings. Just as he did, a commotion in the corridor caught our attention.

"I've got to see Hugo!"

I heard the booming voice of my big brother, Douglas, and so did McGregor. He rose from his desk with an annoyed expression on his face just as Douglas flung open his door. McGregor went from being annoyed, to furious, in an instant. My brother was a big powerful guy, The Dark Prince was his nickname in the posh boarding school we'd attended. Rugby was his game, and that was a sport in which he excelled, being the bruiser that he was. Hence, the officers trying to stop him didn't stand a chance against Douglas' determination to enter McGregor's office.

"What exactly are you doing?" McGregor shouted as he pointed a stern finger at Douglas. With his open-necked shirt and loosely-worn tie, Douglas looked rough. Both his suit and trench-coat looked like he'd been wearing them for a long time. His dark hair, normally slick and neat, was now rather dishevelled and his designer stubble a lot longer than usual. His dark eyes darted anxiously between McGregor and me. I didn't know quite what to feel, sometimes I loved the guy, other times I hated him; at that moment, I couldn't decide. I wasn't surprised that he'd forced himself into McGregor's office. Procedure and protocol weren't really part of his skill set. Had the said circumstances been different, I would've enjoyed this spectacle.

"Sorry Detective Inspector, but I need to speak to my brother, now."

Douglas' demand cut through the voices of the police officers, who were seeking permission from the Inspector to remove the big man. McGregor raised his hand and told his colleagues to leave us alone. Reluctantly they did so. McGregor kept his eyes on Douglas as he waited for the door to shut.

"Detective Sergeant Storm, just exactly who do you think you are?"

McGregor's tone was surprisingly empathetic towards my brother, considering what had just happened. Both men were big, but my brother was younger and fitter and in a fight he would win hands down. I always told myself that, on a good day, I could beat him, but this wasn't a good day. Douglas didn't reply straight away. I could see him searching for something to say to get the desired result: namely to get me out of that police station. I assumed he'd heard about Emily, and that suddenly made it important for me too. I was being a bit slow here.

"Inspector, please, my brother's daughter has been abducted. Sitting here talking isn't going to find her. I know this is procedure, but time is of the essence and we need to be out there searching for Emily."

Douglas spoke calmly, appealing to McGregor to look past protocol, although he could've formulated his request somewhat more diplomatically. Telling the man he was wasting time wasn't really that clever. I looked back at the Inspector who was, to his credit, quelling his anger and considering Douglas' request. I hoped that he was big enough not to focus purely on Douglas' blunt formulation. McGregor was a legend in Scottish law enforcement circles but so too was my brother. Douglas Storm was a hard-hitting officer who also got results. Even though Internal Affairs seemed to lurk in Douglas' shadow on an almost permanent basis, the man carried clout and that mattered to me now. And Douglas had started his police career in Lothian and Borders Police, so McGregor knew him; the question was, how did that knowledge affect McGregor's opinion of the man? Douglas too had his fair share of enemies, and they also included many of his colleagues.

"Okay, brothers Storm! We can do this another time – go with your brother, Hugo – keep in touch and don't step over the line! You hear?" McGregor rasped, and sat back down heavily.

I felt as if I'd been spoken to by a stern headteacher, but I ignored that. It was big of him to do this; if the top brass got to know, it could earn him a severe reprimand. Douglas looked at me and gestured to the door as we both voiced our gratitude.

"Go and find Emily!" the big man exclaimed as he waved us away from his office.

Douglas was silent as we left the almost deserted police HQ, and looking at my watch, I realised it was nine p.m. already. I kept my own counsel as I hurried to stay alongside my brother. Not being one with patience to wait for lifts, Douglas took the staircase down. Outside, the miserable evening continued, a drizzling rain that only Scotland in a foul mood was capable of producing. It didn't register on my radar though. Emily had been missing now for just about seven hours, and what horrors had my little girl experienced?

Douglas had parked right in front of the central entrance. He headed straight for his car.

"What's going on, Douglas?" I enquired as I got in the front passenger seat. He didn't reply, but fired up the mean V8 of his black BMW M5. I laid my hand on his shoulder and leaned over,

"You gonna answer me, or what. No flaming' games, Douglas. Emily is missing!"

Douglas slotted the gear lever into reverse and looked over at me. His face hard and dark.

"Listen Hugo, I damn well know that, okay. Just wait – gonna take you somewhere," he replied with attitude.

Douglas' fuse had always been short, but his rage took me aback for a moment. I retracted my hand but kept my stare on him. Maybe I could take him on a bad day too? He reversed quickly, flipped the gear lever in drive, floored the accelerator and the powerful car took off with spinning back wheels. A couple of police officers getting out of a police van shouted something at us as we tore past them.

"What the hell, Douglas – you aiming to get us arrested again before we've even left?"

I held on for dear life, but Douglas didn't answer as drove on. I felt like punching the man but, with a struggle, managed to hold myself back. Whatever was going on, Douglas wouldn't answer until the time was right. I gathered that it involved Emily, and so I forced myself to sit back and wait. The initial rage, wherever that'd come from, had subsided as Douglas drove a little more sensibly through Edinburgh. We were heading towards the dock area, and after another twelve minutes we entered a poorly-lit street lined

with small-scale storage yards and workshops, some clearly aban-
doned. Douglas killed the lights and drove carefully on, keeping
the engine noise as low as possible. I wondered where on earth this
was, as I looked around. Then just as I was about to demand an answer, we rolled into a small yard. There was no light there and no-
one around.

"Is Emily here?" I whispered as I strained my eyes to look
around.

My insides were in utter turmoil. Anxiety within me was rising
fast. The thought of looking at the dead body of my 12-year-old
daughter made me feel weak and panic-stricken. Douglas cut the
engine and quietly climbed out of the car.

"Come with me, Hugo and keep the noise down."

He didn't wait for me, so I got out as quickly as I could – maybe
she wasn't dead ...

"When are you gonna answer me, Douglas?"

I repeated my question a little louder as I followed him into a
one-storey house-like building.

"Just shut up and come with me," Douglas snapped, walking
on.

The building had long been deserted – no evidence of recent
human activity. There was stuff – rusty machines of some sort and
dust-covered junk everywhere, it was like a derelict workshop. It
must've been months, if not years, since anybody had worked here.
We entered through another door and into a very dark room. I
could smell something that made an alarm go off loud and clear in
my head. It was so dark I couldn't see Douglas, and a bone-chilling
thought struck me like lightning. She was dead – I was being led to
Emily's dead body.

Suddenly a light came on and flooded the room in a stark cold light. I looked around, at first disorientated, with a rage about to boil. Then I saw the body. A dead person laid on his/her back on the dirty floor. Was it Emily, my Emily? I felt faint and had to take a few steps to steady myself. I swore under my breath as I looked intently … it was a man's body! Just what was going on here? Douglas was standing behind me, leaning against a wall. He was standing there with his hands buried in his trench-coat looking at the dead guy on the floor. I rushed over, grabbed Douglas and lifted my clenched right fist ready to punch him in the face. I saw nothing in his dark eyes as he stared back at me. I didn't care, I needed answers, or I'd go for him like a wounded animal.

"Why the hell have you brought me to a murder scene, Douglas?"

My teeth were firmly gritted, barely letting the words pass.

"I killed that guy earlier today," Douglas said in a flat voice devoid of any emotion, as he pointed at the guy.

I shook my head in disbelief. I wanted to go crazy and punch the life out of that guy, my brother. I struggled to hold back my punch as a tirade of emotion burst forth.

"So what? Sorry, but I don't give a damn about that, okay. Why on earth did you bring me here? Emily's missing! I thought that dead body was hers at first! You selfish swine!"

"The stiff was called Jason Stewart, an up-and-coming drug dealer – ambitious bloodsucker – connected."

Douglas paused as he brought out a mobile phone from his trench-coat pocket. He ignored my twisting grip on his coat and my furious nodding as my anger raged.

"Get to the point, Douglas," I hissed.

He worked the screen of the mobile phone and then showed it to me. There, right in front of me, was a photo of Emily, her smiling face looking straight at me, clear as day.

"What exactly is this?" I demanded.

"This isn't my mobile phone, Hugo."

Silence, as I tried to digest what he'd just told me.

"Say again?"

"This here is his mobile," Douglas elaborated as he pointed at the dead guy.

I blinked, trying hard to make sense of something nonsensical. Douglas recognized my confusion and spoke again, his voice still devoid of any emotion.

"I only saw the photo after I shot him."

Douglas' voice trailed off as he looked down, his dark eyes seeing nothing but the abyss. I let go of his coat and grabbed the mobile from his hand, staring at the image of my daughter.

"This is insane! Why in the world does this guy have a picture of my Emily on his mobile phone?"

My thoughts swirled in a total muddle within my head. Emily looked so happy; her face was lit up as only hers could be. She was looking straight at the camera, as if she knew and trusted whoever was taking the picture.

Douglas grabbed my shoulder, demanding my full attention, as he looked at me with eyes laden with pain.

"It's a camera picture Hugo – not a text or email image. Do you get it? That photo of Emily was taken by someone using this mobile camera!"

A silence lingered as I tried to process what he'd just told me. I shook my head again, this didn't make any sense.

"What's this all about Douglas? You'd damned-well better start talking brother! Who was this guy and more importantly, why the hell is there a photo of my little Emily on his mobile?"

"I don't know, Hugo. I know this must be brutal, but I needed you to see this guy and there's no nice way to take somebody to a corpse whose brains have been blown out."

Douglas paused, took another long hungry pull on his cigarette, then killed the glow of the stub with his fingers and dropped it into his jacket pocket before continuing.

"As I said, the corpse was a scumbag called Jason Stewart, who was an ambitious criminal and a long-standing informer of mine. We had a meeting this morning concerning some pressing business and, as you can see, it ended badly. I ended up killing the guy."

He said this in a deadpan voice, before pausing to quickly fire up another cigarette with his old-style metal-cased Zippo lighter. I didn't reply, just took my time processing all the information provided by Douglas and the crime scene we were standing in. Okay, Douglas had killed a guy, execution style, but I couldn't care less to be honest. The only point of interest to me was how the dead guy was linked to Emily.

"Yeah, I know what you're thinking, Hugo," Douglas violently ruffled his greasy hair and continued, "And I'm sorry, brother – but I don't have a clue why there's a photo of Emily on his mobile. Had I known then, I'd have kept him alive and, trust me, I would've gotten the answer even if I'd had to cut his balls off! Damn! I only heard about Emily after I'd shot the guy. Oh, man! Hugo, you know I love Emily." Douglas stopped, visibly shaken, and fought a rush of emotions; a couple of fat tears rolled down his weathered face as he looked me hard in the eyes. I believed his story and I knew he and Emily had a special relationship. Somehow, they'd bonded and developed a truer relationship than Douglas had ever had with anybody else, including his bitter wife and daughter. Remembering that made me soften a little.

"Okay, Douglas, somehow this dead guy was linked to Emily. Lay it out man, about you and him."

I was looking at Douglas intently. Whatever crazy thing had gone down here, I had a lead if I could only find out why this guy had a photo of Emily on his mobile. I looked at the phone again and saw it'd been snapped, and not received as a message, last Saturday at two thirty-seven in the afternoon. A certain chill settled in my spine as I remembered that I'd had Emily that afternoon. We'd had a day together, just her and me. We had some retail therapy, as Emily called it, at Ocean Terminal. We watched a movie that Emily loved, and I pretended to love. Then we lunched and milled about in the city centre for a few hours. She'd been with me all the time I reckoned, except for a few occasions when she or I used the toilet and once or twice when we got away from each other. I looked hard at the dead guy and couldn't remember seeing him at any point during that Saturday. The picture seemed to have been taken outside, but the background was too blurred to place. I calculated the distance between the mobile and Emily to be about two meters, around six feet. I studied the picture and it was terrifying, she was looking straight at the lens and smiling happily and confidently. It looked to me like she knew the guy who'd taken it. Heavens above! What on earth had happened? The panic guy was back, screaming at full volume inside my brain.

"Hugo, Jason Stewart used to work for Cameron Bullard. I say 'used to' because the whispers on the street said the man was going solo. We didn't get far enough for him to confirm this to me before

I ended him." Douglas' voice cut through the mess in my head and brought me back.

"Cameron Bullard!" I snapped back, taking a big breath of air.

"Yup, Jason had climbed the ranks in the Bullard Organisation, reaching the dizzy heights of Head Enforcer! Maybe the boy reckoned he was made for bigger and better things, and was going to go solo ... you okay, Hugo?" Douglas checked on me with a scrutinising look.

I felt like the room had started to spin faster and faster. Was this part of the 'consequences' Cameron had threatened me with?

"I owe Cameron Bullard money," I spat out the words and tried to steady myself.

"What ... you owe Bullard money?"

I felt weaker than ever. Ashamed as well. Had Emily been kidnapped due to my greed and irresponsibility? Was my little girl paying the price for my weakness? It appeared so. I nodded in reply and forced myself to look at my brother.

"Yes, a lot of money."

My voice was cracking up. Now it was Douglas' turn to grab me. His grip on my shoulder was fierce but I hardly felt it.

"What are you telling me, Hugo! How much money do you owe?"

"Thousands, just over a hundred grand, including change and interest! Oh, man, what have I done?" Saying the amount made the hair stand erect on the back of my neck.

"Gambling?" Douglas' voice was filled with anger and his grip on my shoulder tightened further.

"Yeah, there was this weekend about four months ago. Argument with Helena and feeling sorry for myself. I went crazy ... Stupid idiot!" My words sounded really pathetic. I had caused this.

"Yeah, you are a stupid idiot," Douglas confirmed and took a step away.

"For crying out loud, Hugo! A hundred thousand pounds and change. And you thought Cameron Bullard would just let that slide?"

> I didn't reply, I didn't have a reply, I just stood there looking at the dead guy.

"Well, for a criminal, Cameron Bullard is a decent guy," Douglas observed as he came up beside me and looked at the dead guy.

"What do you mean?" I asked, my brain was in chaos; thinking clearly was difficult.

"If he's got Emily, he won't hurt her, wouldn't make sense if he did," Douglas paused before continuing, "No, I don't think Cameron Bullard would allow that."

I shot Douglas a glance and felt the internal mayhem subsiding as I grasped this hope with a vengeance. Yes, Douglas was right, Cameron Bullard wouldn't hurt a little girl. The man himself was a father of six! I knew that as I'd done jobs for his kids earlier in my fixer career. And apparently, he was a good father and a dedicated grandfather too. This hope was immediately attacked by the panic guy though.

"You sure, Douglas... he wouldn't let Emily be hurt?" Each word had to be forced out as I sought his reassurance.

Douglas shook his head.

"No, I'm not sure, but Cameron Bullard is, first and foremost, a business man. He's focused on the end-game, which means getting his money and walking away from this with minimal consequences." Douglas looked over at me and I felt the intensity of his stare.

"What, Douglas? Why are you staring at me?" I asked.

"Do you have the money?"

"Well, in assets, yes, but not in cash."

I felt like an idiot. Had I honoured my debt, then this wouldn't have happened. Douglas didn't reply, just gave me a serious look as he chewed over my simple answer.

"Right, we can fix this," he said, decisively.

The glint of hope was slowly returning to my eyes as I resolved to speak to Mr Bullard as soon as possible. Maybe I could fix this quickly and get my Emily back within the next few hours? That possibility filled me with hope, albeit a fragile one.

"What about the dead guy?" I asked as I glanced down at the body.

"You see that tank?" Douglas gestured towards what looked like a copper tank of some description. I hadn't really noticed it until then. It was filled with some liquid and it dawned on me that it was an acid bath. Oh, Lord! What on earth was going to happen?

"Steady brother, it was meant for me." Douglas laughed gruffly, deteriorating into a rough coughing fit. I saw craziness rolling around in his eyes and it scared me.

"We throw Jason in, and in 24 hours or so, nobody will be able to identify him. Then we go and get Emily ... Or maybe you have a better idea?"

I didn't. I looked at this crazy man who was my brother and nodded my agreement to his macabre plan. What else could I do?

SEVEN

I REFUSED POINT-BLANK to help Douglas dispose of the body. Manhandling the dead gangster into an acid bath was his problem. The last thing I wanted, was to be in any way linked to this crime. I'd been here, yes – but I didn't know what was going on until I arrived, and I hadn't actively assisted Douglas to commit the crime. True, I wasn't going to report the crime, but I assumed any half-decent lawyer could get the charge against me reduced to a minor one, should it come to court. Nonetheless, I hoped that wouldn't ever happen, but if it did, at least not until I'd got my Emily back.

Douglas was certain that, as long as the body wasn't discovered within the next 24 hours, not even the most advanced forensic technology would be able to identify him. He was also certain that nobody knew Jason was meeting him. I could buy that; most criminals don't advertise to their partners in crime that they meet up with cops. But you never know, he might've told somebody about Douglas as an insurance ticket or plain old revenge in case Douglas ended him. I loved my brother, well some of the time anyway, and he was flesh and blood, but I wasn't prepared to go down with him on this, if it came to that.

"You're on your own on this, Douglas!"

After taking stock of the situation, I said it straight to his face. To his credit, Douglas took it without protesting. He shrugged and told me to wait in the car.

After I left the building I took my time looking around. There was an eerie silence, or at least that's how it felt. I used all my senses, listening and looking, just like I'd done during my first and only intel tour in Northern Ireland, when there was widespread fear that the troubles would kick off again.

To my relief, there was no-one around and no vehicles passed by on the road. I felt restless, I wanted to be away, away from this macabre scene, but primarily to go and get my girl back. I fished out my mobile and swiped the screen, debating with myself whether I should call Helena. I decided not to; she would hear the distress in my voice and I didn't want to tell her anything I shouldn't. I knew I needed a little more time before calling her. And that needed to be when I was away from here. I walked down to the entrance of the small yard and stood in the shadows. From here I could view the road both ways.

Lost in my own thoughts, I heard the door open. I turned and saw Douglas at a distance; he was looking for me since I wasn't by the car. I took out my mobile, kind of cupped it with my left hand and aimed the screen at him. Noticing the light, he came towards me, moving surprisingly light-footedly for such a big man.

"Seen anything?"

He was excitedly checking the road as he spoke, the whites of his eyes radiating madness. He reeked of the rank toxic acid, forcing me to step away; it was the smell of death.

"Nothing – we ready to go?" I urged.

"Yeah, let's get out of here!"

Douglas headed back to car without looking at me.

"I'll wait here. Make sure the coast's clear ..."

I held back from telling him to keep the lights off.

"Good idea!"

I watched my brother, a man who'd just killed someone, and I couldn't help but wonder if he'd killed before. The thought sent a shiver down my spine. I knew one thing for certain: I didn't want to know.

"Have Bullard or any of his associates contacted you since Emily went missing?"

Douglas broke the silence as we drove away from the docks, and I suddenly realised something – something very important.

"I'm using a new phone today! Only Helena and Petite have got the number – well, now Inspector McGregor has too."

My brain jolted back to life. It was time to snap out of the numbness and get back to work. Douglas didn't comment but I noticed his jaw tighten. My mind was working on a new scenario: Cameron Bullard and his associates had taken my little girl to get their money back. Pretty hard-ball stuff. Doubts were filling my mind.

"You really think Bullard and crew have taken Emily?"

I needed Douglas' engagement with this situation, but he took his time, chewing it over before replying.

"I don't know, Hugo. I've never heard of Bullard doing anything like that before. If he has, then he's playing with fire, and although he's a risk taker, first and foremost he's a thinking man. That's how he's avoided serving time for the past twenty years."

Douglas chewed on this some more. I agreed with his analysis – kidnapping a little girl to settle a gambling debt was a high-risk move. But the man was a criminal, ethical conventions weren't included in his rule book.

"He'd know the police would be all over this and therefore he wouldn't get directly involved himself. As a rule, Bullard operates under the radar. I know the man wants to retire to the sun ..." Douglas glanced over at me and added, "You must've really rattled his cage!"

I avoided Douglas' eyes, just kept looking straight ahead. I'd been dodging Bullard and the debt for months. And I'd beaten up a couple of his thugs who'd come calling a couple of weeks ago, beaten them up badly in fact. That was just over a week before the acid bather had snapped that photo of Emily. Without doubt, I had rattled his cage!

"Yeah, I must've ..." I started and stopped.

I could see it now: I knew that one of the thugs that I'd beaten to a pulp was a nephew of the old man. That realisation hit me hard. After the event, there'd been an ominous silence for a few days, and when Bullard did contact me, he didn't mention his nephew. But I knew, and he knew.

"Must've what Hugo?"

"I really think I annoyed him a lot. It may be personal." I swallowed hard.

Douglas didn't reply, just indicated and parked the BMW at the side of the road.

"What do you mean; it may be personal?"

Douglas flipped the gear stick into neutral and turned to face me.

"A couple of weeks ago I beat up one of his nephews and another henchman who came calling."

"Who was the nephew?" Douglas asked, with a smile he couldn't suppress; violence excited him, always had, always would.

"Uh, Jack Bullard."

"You raving idiot! You beat up Jack Bullard?"

Douglas shook his head in disbelief, his smile had gone. He looked straight ahead, deep in thought. My thoughts too, were swirling around my head; beating up that guy sure didn't feel like anything to be proud of now. In retrospect, I saw that it was plain stupid, bad judgement, on my part.

"Tell me what happened," demanded Douglas.

"They came calling at my office just before closing time. I let them in and Jack started swaggering about. He and his sidekick were really enjoying themselves, making all kinds of threats towards Helena, my kids, even Petite. Acting as proper imbeciles," I paused, and took a deep breath before continuing, "I lost my temper, I was stressed before those fools turned up anyway. I grabbed the baseball bat that I keep in my office and started swinging it at them. They didn't stand a chance."

There was silence as Douglas contemplated what I'd told him.

"Damn ... okay ... how badly did you beat them? How did you get rid of them?"

"They could walk – well kind of. But neither were going to be using their arms and hands for a while, for a long while. I was driven by rage and literally threw them out. Petite called somebody who came and picked them up off the street afterwards. Nobody appeared to have witnessed it. If anybody did see it, they looked the other way and ignored it. No police came calling. I was surprised."

I returned to my thoughts as Douglas mulled over what I'd just said. I remembered how, after it'd happened, my pulse was racing, but Petite had taken charge and got those thugs lifted off the street outside. She was, as always, calm, efficient and solution-oriented. I didn't know who the clean-up guys were. I'd watched from my office window as they arrived in a van, both wearing masks. They got the beaten-up thugs into their van without any trouble. I didn't ask any questions; Petite knew a lot of people. Then she made coffee and called a cleaning crew, who came and sorted my office. I recalled the way she'd looked at me before leaving for the evening, but the day afterwards it was as though nothing had happened. Business as usual. I told Douglas this and again he couldn't help but smile.

"Petite Williams – one amazing young lady!" he laughed out loud.

We sat for a while in silence. Then Douglas smiled strangely; the madness had returned to his eyes. I could feel his anger igniting within.

"What, Douglas, what is it?"

"I'm just glad I'm not the only one with a lack of self-control."

"Glad you're finding it funny!"

Douglas turned and slapped my shoulder. "Sorry – I'm being totally selfish here. What happened when you spoke to Bullard next?"

"The guy acted as if nothing had happened – surprised me to be honest. I thought all hell would break loose, but no. Bullard told me his patience was coming to an end – in his business-like way."

I had successfully quelled the urge to hit Douglas in response to his mocking tone. Oblivious to my inner struggle, he stroked his unshaven jaw, his smile now gone.

"Classic Cameron Bullard, that. He leaves grandstanding to fools. But you know you've now got an enemy there, brother. You know that, right?"

"Yeah, I'm an idiot. This gambling debt just got out of control. I always found an excuse not to pay him back. Became arrogant. Damn..."

If I had thought Douglas would console me, then I was wrong.

"Definitely – you are an idiot! Just what were you thinking? You've crossed the line with that man. Nobody does that. Anyway, where are Helena and the kids?"

"Not home, out, somewhere safe, I hope!"

I clenched my teeth; I was so angry with myself – my head felt like it was going to explode any minute.

"You hope? Come on – get a grip, Hugo – you must know?" Douglas barked his reply.

"Leave it, Douglas," I fired back, "Petite's sorting them out. Helena's smart, she and the kids have gone underground."

The tension between us was rising fast. Douglas held his breath. I felt the intensity of his anger and wondered what he'd do next. He rolled his eyes and clamped his big hands onto the steering wheel; he was working through the rage, trying to regain his composure.

"Okay, okay. Let's calm down here."

Douglas was telling himself more than me. He took another breath and let it out slowly. Steadied himself. Impulse controlled.

"You're right, both Petite and Helena are capable and smart ..."

Douglas' words whistled out as he scratched his oily hair. My mind was scrambling to find a plan, a solution; I needed to get on top of this. This cluster of almighty mess was my doing – I needed to sort it. I got my mobile out and worked the screen.

"What are you doing?" Douglas asked sharply.

"Calling Helena."

"Okay. Does she know what's going on here?"

"Kind of ..." I replied.

Douglas' cold intense stare demanded more.

"She knows Emily's been kidnapped. She knows bad things are happening, but she doesn't know about Cameron Bullard and the gambling debt."

Douglas reacted to this bombshell by fishing for another cigarette. He lit it and glanced over at me.

"Okay then, you gonna call her, or not? They must be somewhere. Its past midnight – the kids must be sleeping."

"Yeah," I replied absently.

I worked the screen on my mobile again. The number rang. It continued to ring. I felt my heart rate speeding faster. She could be sleeping, but ... Then, to my great relief, a sleepy voice answered.

"Hello, darling,"

Helena's voice sounded just wonderful and I almost started to cry. I kept it together.

"It's just me. You guys sleeping?" I asked.

I deliberately didn't ask where she was. I didn't trust anything at the moment – even the wretched mobile.

"Well, I was – the others are. We are in ..."

"Don't tell me – not now," I cut her off short, "But you guys are safe?"

"What's going on, Hugo. Don't you want to know where we are?" Helena's voice was suddenly awake.

I searched for words – something that wouldn't alarm her more than necessary, but I couldn't find any.

"I don't trust anything just now. I know it's crazy, but I don't have time to explain. As long as you guys are safe then that's what matters. You trust me?" The last words stung me as I said them.

"Of-course I do darling. Don't be silly. Okay. I get you. Any news on Emily?"

Her voice sounded anxious. Again, I carefully considered what I was going to say. I decided she needed a little hope, she deserved a little hope.

"We've got a lead – a very interesting lead, but I can't say more about it just now."

"Oh, that's great. You go and get her, Hugo! You hear?" Then she added, "Who are we?"

"Douglas and me. We're searching for Emily together!"

I knew Helena had a complicated relationship with Douglas, just like the rest of the world. His dark side terrified her, but she could also see his better attributes and she knew he and Emily were close. Helena could cut through nonsense like no other, she knew very well that if anyone could get results on this, it would be Douglas.

"That's great. Tell Douglas I'm counting on him."

I glanced over at my brother, he was keeping silent, but I could see a satisfied smile on his lips. He'd heard.

"Okay Hugo. I'm with Petite anyway, she's sorting everything."

"Right then baby – kiss the kids for me in the morning and, until I give you the green light, don't return home. Stay safe." I felt the love inside me swell up. "I love you so much, Helena. Tell Petite I'll call her later."

"I love you too, darling. Good night."

Helena terminated the call. I stared at the screen for a moment.

"You've got a good woman there, Hugo," Douglas said quietly.

I looked over at him and nodded in agreement. Yes, she was more than I deserved, that was the absolute truth.

"I know, Douglas. She's one in a million."

I put the mobile down, and we sat silently contemplating the situation. Then Douglas rolled his powerful shoulders, grabbed my arm and squeezed it.

"Right, let's find Emily." He squeezed harder in his determination.

I felt a mysterious energy within me. Let's find Emily. Damn right! Just as I was about to reply, blue lights flashed through the cabin of the BMW from behind. We both turned to look. What now?

EIGHT

EMILY'S DISAPPEARANCE had become news. The Police Sergeant who'd been manning the Communication Desk of Police Scotland HQ informed me that a brief press statement had been released. He further confirmed that local and national news media had started to react and were making enquiries. I wasn't exactly sure how I felt about that situation, but I was angry that the press statement had been released without my knowledge and consent. The sergeant couldn't really comment further other than to say, according to the paperwork he had, the family had signalled their consent. Claire must've given the green light without consulting me. Anger flared up inside me until I remembered that Claire didn't yet have my new mobile number.

"You okay, Hugo?" Douglas asked as he got back in the BMW.

The police car behind us pulled out and drove off, honking their horn as they passed us. Douglas flipped them a thumbs-up out of the window. The police officers had noticed the menacing BMW with a couple of guys just sitting there, and had made a routine stop. We'd both got out and approached the police vehicle, gave them a little scare as well. When they realised Douglas was a cop, and who I was, they relaxed. They told me about the news statement concerning Emily. I thanked them and went back to the car. I needed a little privacy, the trauma was still fresh and raw. Douglas hung back and chatted with the uniforms. The man had killed a guy just a few hours ago, dumped the body into an acid bath, and now was talking to his police colleagues as if nothing out of the ordinary had happened. Douglas Storm, a cold fish indeed. I couldn't care less, to be honest.

"Yeah, I'm fine. Just hold on for a moment there, Douglas ..."

I got my mobile out and sent a brief text to Claire. It was carefully worded, she was being torn apart every single second that Emily was missing, I didn't want to be mean. It wasn't her fault I hadn't given her my mobile number. I assumed she could be sleeping, so I didn't wait for a reply. At least she had my number now. I put the mobile down and looked back at Douglas.

"What now?" I asked.

"Let's see if we can find Jack Bullard?" Douglas worked his knuckles as he said this.

"Yeah, you know where he lives?"

"Sure do, he and Jason were close. They live – well lived – in the same block, same floor, opposite side of the landing."

"Right, let's go."

I rolled my shoulders and stretched my arms to ease the stress. Douglas winked and quickly moved through the gears as he floored the accelerator. The back wheels got traction and threw us forward. I didn't comment – just held on as Douglas drove.

"Where does he live?" I asked as we headed east on Ferry Road.

"Not far from Central Prison," Douglas replied and laughed.

I tried to break a grin, but couldn't. It was kind of funny, but smiling for me just felt wrong. I felt guilty as it were, humour just felt totally inappropriate just now.

"What's the plan?"

I already had an idea of what Douglas was planning and consequently I couldn't help but feel that chill down my spine again.

"We'll grab him and make him talk," Douglas answered after a brief silence.

I nodded, my mouth went dry and my tongue felt like it was glued to the roof of my mouth. Make him talk! Douglas sensed my anxiety and glanced over.

"I'll do this, Hugo. If that's okay with you?"

It was a rhetorical question. He focused back on the driving before speaking again. I just waited silently.

"Listen Hugo, time is crucial here. You can't just call Cameron Bullard and say, 'Hi, sorry for being an idiot. I'll pay now – just give me my daughter back and we'll forget all about this.' That's just not gonna happen. I don't know what role Cameron has played in all of this, assuming he is involved,"

Douglas paused, allowing his brain to process the rush of thoughts – it was working overtime. I kept my own counsel, digesting what he'd told me. I knew he was right. I just needed him to say it, needed him to lead the way.

"We don't really know what on earth's going on here. Right? What we do know is that you owe Cameron Bullard a load of money and you've been messing him around as well as beating his nephew up. Then we know that the scumbag I ended yesterday had a picture of Emily on his phone, for no good reason I can think of. But we know this scumbag used to work for Cameron Bullard and was best friends with Jack Bullard. This has got to be linked."

I nodded – it made sense. I still didn't look at my brother. He let out a sigh. He knew that I wasn't going to take the lead here. Maybe I was being a coward, but I knew where Douglas was going with this. I wanted Emily back more than anything else and, if I had to, then I would make this Jack Bullard talk. But I wanted Douglas to say that he would do it.

"And I will make this guy talk. You don't need to be involved. Okay? If anything comes back from this, I'll take the fall myself."

Douglas' words had reassured me. We drove the rest of the way in silence. My mind was racing away. What if this guy had answers? I prayed he did have answers! Whatever it took, really. I brushed off the timidity I'd initially felt, worrying about having already caused this guy harm. What was I thinking? I glanced over at Douglas, and felt a sense of gratitude. He would do what needed to be done, and face the consequences alone if it came to that. I knew he wasn't lying about that.

Arriving at our destination, Douglas headed into a street and found a gap between two cars. He neatly parked the BMW and turned off the lights.

"Here we are," he said pointing his index finger like a gun at the block behind us.

I looked around, it was 3 a.m. The block stood close to a major road, a busy city residential area with rows of 3-storey apartment buildings. Some would be social housing, others privately owned. The point was, the chance of somebody being awake, even at this hour, would be high.

"Okay, what floor does he stay on?" I asked whilst keeping a sharp lookout.

"Top floor," Douglas answered and grimaced, displaying his dissatisfaction.

"Right, if he's home, we've got to lure him away, and without a fuss. Drama here wouldn't be good."

"I hear you, brother,"

Douglas spoke as he leaned between the seats and picked up the bag he'd carried from the warehouse. His body odour was rank, but I ignored it.

"What're you doing?" I asked.

Douglas ignored me as he looked through the bag before pulling out a mobile phone. It was Jason's mobile – the one with Emily's photo on it. He held up a finger to quieten me, as he worked the screen. I waited. It rang and rang repeatedly before anybody answered. Douglas abruptly terminated the call and quickly sent a text message. He turned his attention to me.

"Right, I think that was Jack answering the call, sounded as if he was sleeping. I've just sent him a text, as Jason, telling him to come out and meet me here. Said he'd got some pressing business to discuss."

"You know he's home?"

"No, but we'll soon find out. Listen, you get behind the wheel. I'm heading out. If he appears, I'll snatch him and bundle him in the back. Then you drive off. Got it, Hugo?" Douglas' expression was as grim as his words.

I nodded, "Got it."

I kept an eye on Douglas through the wing mirror as he walked across the road. I was getting a decent view up the street, and if Jack was coming, this was the way he'd walk. Douglas hadn't tried to imitate Jason but had cleverly texted after (presumably) Jack had answered the call. It didn't matter that it was 3 a.m., neither of these guys were nine to five workers. The minutes dragged by. I was nervously tapping my knee, telling myself to cool it. Jack would know something was wrong if he couldn't see Jason. Douglas would have to sneak up and grab him fast before he smelled a rat. Just as I was musing on this, I noticed a guy turning the corner and coming down the street. He was wearing an oversized hoodie and, luckily for Douglas, had pulled the hood up restricting his view. His hands were buried in the front pockets of the hoodie. Douglas must've told him to walk all the way down – and by the looks of it Jack seemed to have bought the premise that it was Jason who'd texted him. I kept very still. The BMW was parked in the twilight between two street lights, and thus the cabin was dark. But I knew he'd notice me if he came up beside the car.

"Douglas, where are you?" I whispered under my breath, just as I saw a shadowy figure slide up beside Jack, and in a smooth motion grab him and force him forward. Keeping the momentum going, I stepped out of the car and opened the back door. Douglas had rammed something in Jack's mouth, so he couldn't shout or scream. He tried to resist, but stood no chance. Douglas marched him rapidly towards the car, holding him in vice-like grip. From a distance it could be perceived as a drunk being helped by a mate. Reaching the car, Douglas simply folded Jack into the back seat and slid in beside him. I shut the door calmly, got behind the wheel, started the car and drove away in as relaxed a manner as I could manage. If anybody had been looking at that moment, they wouldn't have seen anything to be alarmed about. The number plates were illegible anyway, thanks to a film Douglas had sprayed on earlier. It looked like dirt. It was one of the reasons the cops had pulled in behind us earlier that night. Douglas had promised to clean the plates and had then promptly 'forgotten' to do it as soon as they drove away.

"You raving madmen ..."

A high-pitched voice rang out from the back seat, followed by a rapid succession of punches and slaps. I heard the sound of muffled low moaning, and glanced in the rear-view mirror. Jack's eyes widened as he recognised me. His face red from the beating. His eyes pulsed with fear. I returned my focus to the road and felt no sympathy. If he was involved in Emily's kidnapping, then this was just the start.

"Shut your mouth, you miserable excuse for a human being!"

Douglas' tone was dark and sinister as he secured, with some industrial-strength tape, the cloth that he'd stuffed into Jack's mouth.

"Where are we going?" I asked.

"Head for the bypass and then the A68. Drive towards Lauder."

After issuing these instructions Douglas relaxed back into his seat, having secured Jack. I raised an eyebrow, I didn't realise Douglas had a place in the Borders region. Then again, there were many things I didn't really know about my brother's affairs, I didn't need to remind myself that I preferred it that way.

"Sure thing," I said and headed for the bypass.

Outside, the miserable Scottish weather continued – sheets of rain falling from a dark almost menacing sky. I kept to the speed limit. There would be Police Scotland traffic cars out and about, and traffic was light at that time of night; I didn't want them picking on us out of boredom. If we were stopped now, explaining Jack's trussed-up presence in the back seat would be tricky!

We drove on for about hour in silence. Passing through a landscape of rolling hills and white sleek wind turbines: the modern look of rural Scotland. Jack made a few early attempts at gaining his freedom, but Douglas' reaction was swift and violent, so Jack quickly learned to sit still.

Approaching the rural village of Lauder, Douglas leaned forward.

"In about half a mile there's a narrow road on the right, that's where we're going. Okay?"

"Got you," I replied and eased off the accelerator.

The rain was pouring down and visibility wasn't exactly perfect. A thought hit me: this was a performance car, not made for rough tracks.

"Is that road paved – this car won't do any mud wading, you know?" I warned as we approached the turn off.

"I know, the road is paved and it'll be okay," Douglas answered.

There were no cars in front or behind as I turned off the main road. The rain had become even heavier as I slowly drove down the narrow path. Surprisingly, it was in fairly good condition, which was just as well as visibility was becoming even worse. A house suddenly appeared from nowhere. I'd never seen it before, never heard Douglas, his wife or daughter talk about it either. That they didn't know about it wouldn't have surprised me – they knew very little of Douglas' complicated life.

"Where do I park?" I asked.

"Drive around the house, there's a large garage at the back. You can't see it from here."

"Where does this road end?" I asked as I drove around the house.

"Here."

I parked the car in front of a large garage, old but well maintained.

"The keys are in the bag, on a key ring with a metal cross. The garage has a side door – the key is the gold one. You open the door, and I'll follow, okay?"

Douglas gestured for me to get on with it. Normally I would've become highly irritated by his tone, but this wasn't the time to cause friction. I did as ordered: got out of the car and hurried over. There were only a few metres between the car and garage, but the heavy rain soaked me through as I fumbled with the key. Douglas appeared, dragging Jack with him and I followed them in. Douglas flicked the switch, and the stark ceiling light illuminated the space. I looked around and saw a wall covered with various tools, but most interesting was the heavy wooden chair standing in the middle of the floor.

"What the hell." I said as Douglas dragged Jack over, slammed him down in the chair, then shouted to me.

"There're some ropes and belts in the first drawer of that unit – bring them here!"

Jack had recouped some energy, or maybe it was just sheer adrenaline, but he'd decided to fight Douglas. There was a lot of grunting as Douglas held him down. A desperate man can find strength he didn't know he had. I hurried over and opened the large top drawer, got out the rope and some cargo-securing belts and took them over to Douglas. He snatched the rope from me and started to tie Jack down. Jack was howling into the cloth that'd been crammed into his mouth, his face was as red as a tomato and his eyes bulged grotesquely, like in a cartoon.

"Miserable wretch! Here hold him down whilst I get this done," Douglas muttered as he worked fast to tighten the rope.

My heart was racing, this wasn't something I'd ever done before. Jack was fighting now like a terrified, cornered animal, and I had to summon all my power to keep him down in the chair. Where on earth did the junkie get his strength from? Finally, Douglas secured him and used the belts to make certain of the job. Jack was as deflated as a spent balloon. Tears started to run down his face. Douglas walked around him, making sure he was securely restrained, and then looked at me and broke out in a menacing grin.

"Yep, he's going nowhere!" The madness was back in his eyes.

"Just one more thing,"

Douglas took a few steps towards the garage door before reaching up. There was a ceiling-mounted camera that I hadn't noticed. He aimed it at Jack and turned it on. A small green light flickered.

"Let's go to the house. I don't know about you, but I need coffee,"

Douglas spoke in a matter-of-fact way as he walked out, not even looking at me. I hesitated for a moment and surveyed Jack; the whole thing appeared beyond surreal. What exactly was this place?

NINE

I ENTERED THE HOUSE through a side door and quietly walked around. It was ordinary, clean and tidy, minimal furnishings, with the odd picture here and there on the walls. Nothing personal was visible anywhere. The scent of cigarette smoke hung in every room. It felt very cold and neutral. I heard a noise from another room and followed it. Douglas was brewing coffee and slapping together sandwiches as I walked into the kitchen. On the counter was an open laptop, the screen of which presented a live feed of Jack, on the chair, in the garage. The kitchen was in keeping with the rest of the house: functional without any personal touches. It was bland – modern but not fashionable – a place one would find difficult to describe after having left it. Douglas picked up a sandwich and pointed towards the kitchen counter.

"Help yourself, Hugo. There's sugar there and milk in the fridge if you fancy."

I looked at him, wondering if I wanted him to tell me more about this place. The whole scene had been prepared as if he'd planned to bring somebody out here; the chair in the garage and camera zooming in certainly weren't an everyday set up. Douglas wolfed down the sandwich whilst looking at me. I wondered if he was enjoying my obvious apprehensive curiosity. It felt like he was daring me to start digging for information.

"Yeah, I'll have a cuppa," I said lightly and headed for the kitchen counter, ignoring the many questions cascading in my head. I would get to them, eventually, I told myself.

I made my coffee strong, sweet and black, and took it over to the round table. As I sat down I realised just how physically and mentally fatigued I was. The sudden rush of adrenaline had kept me going but it was now ebbing away. I glanced at my silver, metal-chained TAG Heuer wristwatch. It read five to six. Emily had been gone for over fourteen hours now. That thought shifted the fatigue away. I wondered how she'd spent those hours. A chill ran down my spine. I took a sip of the coffee and looked at the laptop. Douglas followed my gaze.

"I'm going to make him talk, Hugo. Don't you worry about that," he said darkly as he looked at the screen, devouring the last of his sandwich.

I was about to tell him how grateful I was when my mobile buzzed. I checked the caller I.D, and swiped the screen to answer, putting on my cheeriest tone.

" Hi Petite, everything okay? Helena and the kids still sleeping?"

"Yeah, I've just checked on them, they're all sleeping – soundly, I might add – together. Good thing it's a super-king-sized bed! It's pretty crowded," Petite laughed lightly.

I let out a sigh of relief. I trusted Petite, and with good reason. Time and time again, she'd proved her trustworthiness, come rain or shine. People always claim to be dependable – but in reality their integrity is usually subject to circumstance, agenda and incentive, but not Petite.

"Thank you, Petite. You know how much that means to me."

"I know. Listen Hugo, it's not a problem ..." she paused, and I could picture her, steeling herself before she continued.

"What's going on? Any development on Emily?"

Her voice was clear, but nonetheless I detected an underlying anxiety. Petite knew Emily well, they'd spent time together and had got to know each other. Emily always told me how cool she thought Petite was, and I knew the feeling was mutual.

"We've got a lead, Douglas and I. Can't talk about it just now. I need you to take care of Helena and the kids for me for the next few days. I'm not sure what's going on here, but I need Helena and the kids to stay under the radar for now. Is that okay?"

"Yes of course. I'll keep us all off the chart. We'll keep moving and stay away from Edinburgh. Make it a fun break for the kids. Don't worry, nobody'll find us, let alone bad guys. I'm Petite Williams, remember! You and Douglas get Emily back. You hear?"

I nodded to her voice, once more full of confidence and unbreakable steel. Strength is a complex thing, not just physical. And Petite Williams had it in spades, with a super-smart brain too. I knew Helena and the kids would be safe. It took a load off.

"Thanks again, Petite. I'll call later. And we will, don't you worry!" I terminated the call.

"Petite's awesome." Douglas said as I looked up from the screen.

"She sure is." I swallowed hard, glancing at the laptop, "Maybe, I should come with you?"

"No, Hugo, you don't want to do that. I'll do things that you don't want, or need to know about ... or to see." Douglas' voice had a strange serenity to it. I could see he was searching for words. I waited.

"Nothing gained by you coming with me ... I'm damaged, Hugo. You know it, I know it. If there is a God, I'm sure I got a one-way ticket to hell! I've done a lot of things I shouldn't have – my weakness for gratification drove me off the cliff a long time ago. But at least I can help get Emily back ..." Douglas looked down, his words hanging out there for both of us to digest.

I lifted my hands in a helpless gesture of brotherly love. I wanted to grab him and give him a hug. But I didn't, I just placed my hands on the table and looked away. The moment passed and Douglas got up. Without looking at me, he turned to leave.

"Wait here," he instructed, as he left the kitchen.

Minutes passed and I couldn't help but look over at the laptop. Douglas appeared in the live stream, said something to Jack, waited for a moment, and suddenly struck him. Douglas had hit him so hard that it looked as if both Jack and the chair would keel over. I jumped back in my chair so fast that I knocked it to the ground, all the while keeping my eyes fixed on the screen. Douglas disappeared for a moment, and then re-appeared holding something in his hand. I moved over and looked hard at the screen. Douglas had some kind of tool in his hand. Was it a wire cutter? I closed the laptop and turned away. Douglas was right, I didn't want to see this. Inside me, nausea mixed with feelings of helplessness. I paced the kitchen, working my knuckles whilst trying to keep things in perspective. I kept telling myself that I didn't object to what Douglas was doing, this Jack character was a nasty piece of work. He had it coming. If he had been involved in Emily's abduction, then he definitely had it coming. I just didn't have the stomach to witness torture, let alone partake in it.

The minutes became an hour, and my pacing continued. I meticulously checked out the house, whilst carefully avoiding the laptop. But my mind was nothing but chaos. At times I heard screams, and the hair on the back of my neck stood up. Then, just under two hours later, I heard the side door creak. I stepped into the corridor and saw Douglas. He looked like a man possessed – like a character from Dante's Inferno; his eyes radiated the madness I'd seen before, but worse. We looked at each other in silence, for what felt like an eternity. I held my breath until I could hold it no longer.

"For crying out loud, Douglas – say something! Tell me! Did the bastard talk?" My voice was fragile, but insistent, filled with pain and fear.

Douglas shook his head and lowered his eyes. Finally, he said, "He didn't know anything".

Something snapped inside me. I spun around and punched the wall; fear and rage exploded from within. Ignoring the pain in my knuckles, I turned back to Douglas.

"You absolutely sure?"

"Yes, he would've spilt the beans if he knew. He pleaded... cried... considering what I did to him. Nobody could have known and not talked, let alone a jumped-up Scottish would-be gangster. He knew Jason was meeting up with me, but not why. I believed him."

I felt deflated – utterly deflated – my legs felt weak. I stepped back into the kitchen and sat down. Douglas followed and sat opposite me. There was blood splattered on his arms, chest and along his jaw line and forehead. I gathered he'd used a face shield and gloves.

"So, what now? I guess Jack's gone?"

Douglas just nodded and leaned back. "I'll get rid of him, Hugo. Don't worry. As I said, if this comes back to haunt us, I'll take the fall." Douglas glanced over at the laptop.

"He did say Cameron Bullard was planning something special for you though. But he denied any knowledge of Emily's kidnapping."

I looked up, that was something. I grabbed it. "Maybe Cameron Bullard organised Emily's kidnapping without Jack's knowledge?"

"Could be. Jack wasn't the sharpest tool in the box, so yeah, very likely," Douglas replied.

"How do we get to Bullard though?"

"With great difficulty – the man's well protected, and if he is involved he'll know we're coming for him."

"Damn," I said and leaned my forehead into my hands.

The hope of a quick rescue was gone. Emily's horror would continue, if she was still alive, that was. My stomach started to churn, and my head thumped like there was a bass drum inside it.

"How long have you been awake, Hugo?" asked Douglas.

"Not sure, more than 24 hours now I guess."

I felt every hour of it etched upon me. My body was aching, the headache splitting my brain into chunks.

"Why don't you have a sleep whilst I sort the garage. You need to be able to think clearly if we're going to find Emily."

"No way," I said and looked hard at Douglas.

"Listen brother, this isn't over by a long shot. I need you to be on the ball when I need to rest. I don't know how much longer I can keep this going, I've been awake for something like 30 hours now. My brain's fried. We continue without rest and we're gonna make big mistakes. Would that help Emily?"

I was about to bark another reply, but I knew he was talking sense. I didn't know how much I would sleep – if I could at all – but I needed to try. Even if I just got an hour or two I'd be able to think straight again.

"Guess there's a bed here?" I gave in to reason and got up.

Douglas nodded and got up too. "Yeah, in the back. The bedding is clean."

"You got any painkillers too?" I asked.

Douglas broke a mean grin and replied, "You're asking me if I've got any drugs? Ha ha! Of course. In the bedroom, top drawer of the cabinet under the window."

He threw me a bottle of still water from the fridge. I managed to catch it, but the effort clearly told me how tired I was.

"Thanks," I said, and shuffled out of the kitchen. "Wake me in an hour – two, tops – okay?"

The bedroom was clean but the air was a little stuffy, so I opened the window. The rain had stopped outside, and fresh cold air flowed into the room. The top drawer of the cabinet resembled a mini-pharmacy. I decided on Co-Codamol, and flushed it down with some water before collapsing on top of the bed.

I did sleep at first but then the image of Emily in a dark, damp cellar came to haunt me. She was cold and scared, at her wits' end. The cellar had no windows, and was bare, other than ... the image was blurry. I couldn't see it, but Emily could; she was looking at it and her entire body was shaking in fear. She was sitting on the dirty floor, chained by her neck to a pole in the middle of the room. Her face swollen by tears, her knees drawn up, arms folded over them, trying to protect herself.

"No!" I gasped from the pit of my stomach, and sat bolt upright like a coiled spring, suddenly released. I couldn't catch my breath at first. I was soaked in sweat and my heart was racing.

"You okay, Hugo?"

A worried voice caught my attention, but I couldn't answer. I swung my legs onto the floor and got up. Douglas put a hand on my shoulder and forced me to look at him. I swayed, trying to pull myself together.

"Emily. I saw Emily – she's in a cellar. A dark cellar, chained to a pole in the middle of the room. There's something else in there; I couldn't see it, but Emily could. She was so scared, Douglas – my little girl was so very scared."

I started to cry. Douglas pulled me in for a hug and held me whilst I sobbed. He didn't say anything, just held me whilst I let it all out. After a while, I stopped, and pulled myself free. I didn't feel awkward; it was natural.

Douglas just stayed there, silently looking at me. Then he said, "We're going to find her, Hugo. Mark my words, we are going to find her and bring her home."

I knew he meant well but his words sounded so hollow, so utterly clichéd. Were we really going to find her and bring her home? Would she still be alive if we found her? If it took weeks or even months, before we found her, and she was – against the odds – still alive, would she be anything else other than a wrecked empty shell? I shook my head, forcing those thoughts away. That train of thought didn't do anyone any good. It certainly didn't help Emily. I wondered about the images in my dream. I'm not a spiritual person, rather, I'm a hardcore pragmatist. But I was desperate enough to be open to anything and everything just now. I looked back at

Douglas. He looked terrible, and he smelled even worse. He read my mind, or did he just notice my disgusted expression?

"Yeah, I'm going to have a shower, then I need a sleep. Give me an hour of shut eye and then we're back on. Deal?"

"Deal, I'll have a shower after you and I'll let you sleep for an hour." I left the bedroom.

The shower had made me feel somewhat human again. I'd slept for a couple of hours and now felt fresh enough to resume the hunt for Emily, but I needed to be patient and let Douglas sleep for a while longer. His snoring was belting out of the bedroom – how could he sleep so soundly after all he'd done? I wandered into the kitchen and noticed the laptop was gone. I didn't look for it. The less I knew about what'd happened here the better.

I made myself a coffee and looked for some food. I needed to refuel. The mobile buzzed, signalling the arrival of a couple of messages, one was from Helen, brief and to the point. 'I love you with all my heart,' it said. I smiled as I fired back a quick reply. I was truly blessed with this beautiful lady.

Then I noticed that the other text was from McGregor. It too was brief and to the point, 'Call me!' I knew that I needed to prepare before complying with that particular order. He would ask where I was, and what Douglas and I had been up to. I needed answers that would satisfy an instinctively-sceptical, veteran, homicide cop. If I told him something that didn't ring true to him, or worse, something which he knew to be a lie, I'd be in big trouble. Inspector McGregor would haul me in. If I had to go on the run, he'd come after me. Then he'd be diverting resources from finding Emily to finding me. I couldn't allow that. He knew Douglas and I were out there, knocking on doors and, if required, knocking heads together too. To a point, I assumed, he would accept that as long as we didn't cross any lines. But we had certainly crossed all possible lines. I sat down and looked at his brief message. I didn't want to tell him where I was; this place had to stay off the police radar. Douglas had kept it from me, so I assumed his police employer didn't know about it either. I knew Douglas had disposed of Jack as best as possible, but you could never be too sure. Even an experienced cop made mistakes. But I couldn't tell McGregor I was in Edinburgh either; if he needed to see me immediately, it'd take me at least an hour to get there. That was one of those lies that could trigger a sceptical mind. 'It's your kid we're talking about, but you can't be here straight away?' I could almost hear him saying that. The safest option was to tell him that I was somewhere else, out of Edinburgh but not in this direction. The possibilities cascaded around in my mind.

I ate my food and drank my coffee, forcing myself to stay analytical. Rushed moves were bad moves. The trick was to make lies as close to reality as possible. Once you started to spin a lie it was easy to get tangled up in it, and before you knew it, total chaos would ensue. I'd learned this the hard way. I tapped the table whilst building my confidence to call McGregor. The knuckles on my right hand were swollen. I flexed my fingers and made a fist, a dull ache pulsed up my wrist. Couldn't be helped. I picked up the mobile and swiped the screen.

"To blazes with it!" I muttered under my breath, and dialled the number. It rang only a few times in reality, but it felt much longer.

"Yes, Detective Inspector McGregor speaking."

"McGregor, it's Hugo. You sent me a text." My voice was under control, for the moment.

"Hugo, thanks for calling back. Where are you?"

Damn! He wasn't wasting any time, was he? I closed my eyes and tried to mentally pin down the cover story I'd devised.

"Stirling way. What's happening?" I hoped he'd move on.

"Stirling? Why?"

"I'm with Helena and the kids. Just catching up with them."

"I see, why are they not at home? Any problems? Sorry for digging."

His voice was light, but I thought I already heard the cogs starting to turn. Or was it just me being paranoid? I pressed on.

"No problem. Helena just wanted to take the kids away for a while. Particularly since this is becoming news now. Now what's up, Detective Inspector?"

I was quite pleased with myself. I'd decided against telling him that I feared for their safety; that would've just invited a potential barrage of questions that I didn't want, not at this stage. A moment passed whilst McGregor considered what I'd just told him. I waited, he needed to let this go himself; if he thought I was pressing him to let this go, those cogs would start turning for certain.

"Fair enough. Ms Munro has tried to get in touch with you. It seems you haven't given her your new mobile number?"

There was a slight accusation in that gruff voice of his. I was sure I had but maybe I hadn't.

"My mistake. I'll call her straight away. Any other news?"

I knew there wasn't any, if there had been, he would've told me by now.

"No, I am afraid not. Rest assured though, we're working at full throttle. I've spoken to Claire, and she agrees with us that a press conference would be a good move. What do you think?"

I took a moment. I couldn't see any good reason why not. It might reach somebody in the know who's nursing some element of remorse or even guilt. Maybe it could result in the police receiving an anonymous call with vital information.

"Yes – definitely. It's a good idea. Any idea when?"

"This afternoon. I can get the media handlers on it straight away. When can you get back?"

"I'll be back in two hours. Is that okay?"

"Yes, just call me on this number when you're back. Oh, by the way, is Douglas with you?" The last sentence was sneaked in there. My paranoia returned with a vengeance.

"Yes," I replied, keeping it short.

"Can you get him on the phone now?" McGregor asked.

I listened intensely, trying to figure out if those cogs were turning.

"No, he's not here just now. I'll get him to call you back the minute I see him again."

Another pause on the other side. I told myself there was nothing in it. Douglas was a police officer and the police wanted to speak to him. Perfectly normal.

"Yes, that'd be great, the sooner the better! Right then, call me when you get back. Speak soon. Goodbye." McGregor terminated the call.

I sat staring at the screen, thinking about that seemingly innocent phrase, 'the sooner the better'. Had they found Jason Stewart? I looked at my watch. The guy had been in the acid bath less than twelve hours. Could they still identify him? More importantly, had we been observed and identified at the scene? Maybe there'd been a CCTV camera that neither Douglas nor I had seen? No, that couldn't be! The conversation with McGregor would've been very different if he'd had the slightest suspicion that Douglas and I had been involved in a murder. He would've pushed me to say exactly where we were, and he hadn't. But Douglas needed to speak to him and I wanted to know why. I glanced at my watch. Douglas had been sleeping for just over an hour; it was time for him to get up. Before I headed back to the bedroom I sent a brief text to Claire. I noticed the message I had sent before had not been delivered.

It took several minutes of my shaking Douglas before he sat up. His breath was repellent. He looked like a wreck, with puffed-up eyes and oily hair standing on end. I guess he needed another shower.

"For pity's sake! What time is it, Hugo?"

He was trying to blink the sleep out of his eyes. Reluctantly, he swung his legs out of bed.

"Nine. Time to get going, Douglas."

"Uh ... Right," he muttered and yawned as he adjusted his underwear, checking his 'credentials' as he did so. It was time for me to leave.

"Inspector McGregor called. Meet you in the kitchen," I said as I left the room.

"Uh ... McGregor ... wait," Douglas shouted after me with a hoarse voice.

TEN

WE WERE HEADING BACK to Edinburgh, Douglas was driving – both of us preoccupied in deep thought. Douglas had called McGregor back, and had been probed about a rumour picked up by an undercover cop the night before. The rumour was going around that a senior drug cop was allegedly involved with a missing associate of Cameron Bullard, named Jason Stewart. Douglas had played well, kept his cool and told McGregor he'd look into it. Even to my ears, Douglas sounded genuine, but I guessed that if one lived a lie, telling lies was easy.

"I'm not sure if I want to know about you and Jason, but what I do need to know is whether you think you're about to be exposed?" I ventured.

I was organising my thoughts, trying to get a handle on this situation. The initial shock had subsided, and my brain was in analytical mode. Jason Stewart had to be linked to Emily's abduction. Why else would he have a photo of my girl on his phone? Who was he working for? I was starting to expand on this thought, maybe it wasn't Cameron Bullard? If not, then who could it be, and why hadn't I heard anything? An idea popped into my head, and I took out my phone just as Douglas answered.

"No, I don't think so. Jack told me yesterday that he knew about the meeting because Jason had told him, by way of an insurance. If he hadn't heard from Jason, Jack was going to shop me in today. Jason thought he had a play choreographed yesterday, but it didn't go according to plan. I killed him before he could tell me about Jack. If he had told me, then there might have been a different outcome. But then again, I wouldn't have seen the picture of Emily ... what are you doing, Hugo?"

"Checking my emails. I haven't done that since Emily was kidnapped."

I logged into my account and waited for a moment for the inbox to upload onto my phone, the signal here was patchy, and it was taking its time.

"Okay."

After saying that, Douglas fell silent. I knew he too was taking a step back, trying to look at this with some perspective.

I noticed that I'd received an email from Ariella Cantor that very morning. I opened it and read:

'Dear Hugo Storm. I have tried to contact you without any success. Both your mobile and office numbers go straight to voicemail. I just want you to know I have, with shock, read the news about the abduction of your daughter, Emily. I am utterly devastated by this terrible news, and my heart goes out to you and your family. I sincerely hope Emily will soon be found – safe and in good health. If there is anything I can assist with, please let me know. You already know this, but if I may say, I know how you feel. Just as I was starting to look into the apparent suicide of my late husband Victor, Chloe was abducted, and my world shattered. Please take care and let me know if I can help in anyway. Yours sincerely, Ariella Cantor.'

I paused and re-read it. She was lovely – without doubt – and I was very grateful for her kind words, but there was something else there. Just as I was starting to gather my thoughts, the mobile buzzed. It was Claire's phone. I hesitated, which didn't go unnoticed by Douglas.

"Who is it?" he asked, without taking his eyes off the road.

"It's Claire's phone," I replied.

"Well, hurry up and answer it then, Hugo. What are you thinking?"

Douglas was right, what was I thinking? I swiped the screen and answered.

"Hello."

"Hi Hugo, it's Claire ..."

Her voice was low and fragile. I could sense her pain and it made my stomach start churning all over again. I realised that was why I'd hesitated, I was trying to get back on an even keel, brain thinking straight and eyes wide open, pumped to hunt for Emily. I shook my head, in an attempt to block the grief-induced paralysis from entering.

"Hi Claire, good to hear from you. Have you slept?" I kept my voice deliberately light and strong.

"Uh ... kind of, mum chased me to bed a few hours ago. She wouldn't take no for an answer ... Have you found Emily yet?" she blurted the words out and started to cry.

My heart was stabbed a thousand times over as I listened to her sobs. I searched for words to comfort her but couldn't find any. Douglas glanced over, he could hear her crying too. His jaw tightened as he focused back on the road. I took a deep inward breath and released it slowly.

"No, but we've got good leads."

It sounded so empty, but it was all I had. I wasn't going to tell her not to cry. How could I, when that was all I wanted to do too.

"Leads? We ...?" she asked, as she regained her self-control.

"Yeah, Douglas is with me. I can't say anything more just now. I'm really sorry, but it is promising!" I paused for a moment before asking, "Listen, is the police liaison officer with you just now?"

Claire would have a police liaison officer with her and he or she would immediately report back to McGregor that we had leads. If they realised a tenth of what we'd been up to, then we'd be closed down. It'd be tricky to explain leads to McGregor without blowing the whole thing. A silence lingered as Claire considered what I'd asked her. She knew Douglas and me well, she could guess what we were doing. Her relationship with Douglas had always been strained; she simply didn't like the man. But she was big enough to allow Emily to have contact with him and she respected the way Emily felt for him.

"No, I'm in the bedroom and she's in the kitchen. What's going on, Hugo?" Her voice sounded a little stronger. I knew I'd given her some hope.

"We're cracking skulls and finding the heartless good-for-nothings who took Emily. But if the police know what we're doing, then they'll stop us straight away. You understand Claire?"

I'd made my mind up. She deserved the truth, well, up to a point. Nothing would be gained by telling her about the actual killings.

"You keep cracking skulls, Hugo! You hear? And tell Douglas I'm behind you both 100%. I don't give a damn what you have to do, as long as you get my daughter back! And I'm not telling the police anything you don't want me to tell them." Her voice was full of determination.

I'd given her hope all right and a certain anger. Anger was better than soul destroying grief. It would give her something to hold on to and maybe she'd remember something that would help Douglas and me, or the police. I'd be more than happy for the police to find Emily first – it wasn't a game. I only cared about Emily, and finding her was the only priority.

"Good, and thank you, Claire."

"Don't thank me, Hugo. You're a good father. I always knew that, but maybe I didn't appreciate that fact in the past. And I love you too, always have and always will ..."

Claire cut herself short. Maybe she felt she'd already said too much? I scrambled about for the right words, I didn't want her to worry about what she'd just said. I cared about her too much to put that on her shoulders too.

"Thank you, Claire for your kind words. I love you too, and always will. You gave me Emily; how could I not love you? Listen, I'll keep you up to date as much as I can." I was moving this on.

"Appreciate that, Hugo," Claire replied. She'd shrugged it off.

"Right then, what do you think about the press conference?"

"Nervous about it, I guess, but I also think it's the right thing to do. If it helps find Emily, it's a good thing, right?"

She needed my reassurance on this, I could tell from her questioning intonation.

"Yeah, I agree. The police know these things. They wouldn't have recommended it unless it made sense. Maybe we should meet before though?" I suggested.

"That's a good idea," she replied enthusiastically. "Why don't you come here first. Then we can head over together."

"Cool, let me speak to McGregor again and I'll call you back. Is that okay?"

"Yes. Call me as soon as you've got something ... Find Emily, Hugo. Find her! Bye."

Claire's parting exclamation rang out intensely as she ended the call. I put the mobile down and checked our current location. We were closing in on Edinburgh. The rain had stopped, and the sky was blue. Under different circumstances that would've made me happy. Now I just noticed.

"How do you do it?" Douglas asked.

"Do what?" I replied, glancing over. What was he talking about?

"Make people love you. Claire left you, but she never ever said anything bad about you. Emily always loved you, fiercely too, even when you got together with Helena and had the younger ones. Helena loves you, despite your great relationship with your ex. I mean, my wife can't stand me. My own kid can't stand me. Even my girlfriends end up hating me ... ah, never mind."

Douglas laughed, but it was a hollow laugh, soaked with bitterness. He looked a little sheepish. I didn't respond, didn't know what to say. Maybe you shouldn't have had so many girlfriends, I thought, but I didn't dare say. We drove on in silence again, thankfully.

Douglas cleared his throat and glanced over, "What now, Hugo? Any ideas?"

"We've got to find Cameron Bullard," I said.

"You mean, find the man, and confront him?" Douglas checked my meaning.

"Pretty much."

"You think he'll throw his hands up and say: 'darn – sorry about that – let me take you to Emily'?"

Douglas' voice carried an element of mocking, which I ignored. I didn't have an exact plan yet. I was extremely anxious about actually meeting the man face-to-face, but if he had my daughter, I was certain I'd be able to tell, even if he claimed innocence.

"What else do we have?" I paused – thinking fast – before continuing, "We can run around in rings here, find another associate of Jason or Jack, and pray he knows something. The problem is, who would that be, for starters? Or we can go straight to the man who would've ordered this, and blow the whole thing up. If he ordered Emily's kidnapping, we'll know – one way or the other."

"It's thin, Hugo, possibly reckless, even counter-productive, but you've got a point."

"I know that, help me then, help us find the angle we need to approach and confront him."

"Right, let me think." Douglas needed time to organise his thoughts – and so did I!

As Douglas drove down the bypass, he kept to the speed limits as his mind was pondering what I'd proposed. A few minutes passed before he looked over.

"You're right, let's blow this up and see what happens." he paused and concentrated on the road before continuing, "You know this might increase the danger for Emily, unless we manage to stop Bullard communicating anything to anyone else whilst we talk to him ..."

I was attempting to pivot my perspective when a thought struck me, "What if we approached, seeking his help?"

Douglas glanced back at me. I could see he was chewing on my new idea. It was still forming in my mind, but the more I thought about it the more I liked it. Every man has an ego, some bigger than others. Cameron Bullard was smart, but he wasn't infallible. I knew his ego was larger than most; a person didn't get to his position and manage to retain it without an inflated view of oneself. I desperately wanted to meet him, as I believed seeing him in person would provide me with insight. I could read people, even a cunning manipulator as clever as Cameron Bullard. If he believed I harboured no suspicion of his involvement, he might give me the clue I needed to confirm to myself that he was indeed involved.

"Yeah, I think you've got something there, Hugo ... I like it," Douglas finally said.

"I think so too. I know it's not perfect, but it's better than going in guns blazing, so to speak." I paused – letting my thought processes continue to work on it. Douglas used the opportunity to spin further on it. He was playing devil's advocate here, and that was fair enough.

"Let's not kid ourselves here though, Hugo. He's a careful man, he might believe we do think he's involved – if for no other reason than for revenge."

"Sure, that's why I've got to do this alone!" I said emphatically.

"No way, Hugo!" Douglas didn't want to be left out.

"Yes, I do. Listen, if we both go, I think he'll be a whole lot more cautious. I've got some history with this guy. I'm pretty sure he'd view you as hostile, even if you kept your mouth shut."

"You go in alone, Hugo, and your back will be totally exposed. I might not be able to get to you in time if this goes nuclear."

"I know. I can look after myself. Anyway, we've got to find the guy first. We might not locate him before the press conference. That reminds me, I've got to call McGregor," I vocalised my thought.

"It's your play. It's Sunday, Bullard will be in one of his pubs, I reckon. We'll head over to his favourite. I'll wait outside in the car. Deal?"

"No, I've got to drive there in my own car. You've got to be at least a couple of blocks away; they mustn't see you. Understand, Douglas?"

I gave him a hard stare. He needed to understand that if Bullard knew he was lurking outside, the chances of this going down in flames would be dramatically increased. I just felt it.

"Okay, I hear you," Douglas replied. That wasn't good enough.

"No, damn it Douglas. You've got to flaming' promise me this. They spot you, and I won't be leaving alive. Don't you dare argue, just do as I say!"

Douglas' jaw went tight and his face went darker. He wasn't used to being spoken to like that. I didn't give a damn about his sensitivities in this case. I just needed him to concede.

"All right, you've got my word. I'll stay away. But you call me the minute you're out and if you believe it's going badly, just bloody call me straight away!"

I nodded in agreement, feeling a great sense of love for my corrupt and damaged big brother. I was also very grateful to him. I knew he would come regardless and throw himself in against all the odds if necessary. It might be too late in some ways, but Douglas could definitely be relied upon in that scenario.

Cameron Bullard fully owned, or held stakes in, several establishments in Edinburgh and beyond. Douglas knew most of them and was certain of where Bullard would spend a Sunday afternoon. The man was in his late sixties and a football fan. Hibernian Football Club was his team, and if Bullard couldn't be at Easter Road Stadium, then he'd be certain to watch the game on TV. He would hang out in a relaxed place with people he was comfortable with. Douglas pointed out a pub which I agreed on. I'd met Bullard there myself, in the past.

Douglas dropped me off outside Claire's where my car was still parked. I'd hoped I could just jump into it and take off, but as I jogged up the street, Tom came out of the house and saw me. He lifted an arm and waved. I had no choice other than to speak to the man.

"Claire's inside. Her mum and sisters are there too."

Tom raised his eyebrows indicating, I assumed, the stress that implied. No wonder the man was leaving. We shook hands.

"Okay, you off?" I asked and pondered the possibility of waiting until he'd gone, and then making a quick escape.

"Yes, got a few things to do ..."

He paused and looked at me as the blood drained away from his face. I knew he was trying to muster courage to ask about Emily. I made it easy for him.

"I don't have any news about Emily – but I haven't given up yet."

I was surprised at how easily those words tripped off my tongue. But I was finished being paralysed by grief and shock, I could fall apart later. Tom nodded and looked down. I knew the man just wanted to escape. I slapped his shoulder in a friendly manner.

"Well, see you later, Tom."

"Yeah, see you later,"

He hurried to his car and as I looked back at the house I saw Claire's mum eyeing me from the front door. There would be no quick escape.

"Hugo, Hugo, come in," she shouted and beckoned to me.

Just under an hour later and I was heading towards the pub where I hoped Cameron Bullard would be. I'd spoken to Claire as well as McGregor, and the press conference was on. McGregor didn't have any good news, the police investigation was going nowhere, but he tried to sound optimistic, more for Claire's benefit than mine. The media event was scheduled for six p.m. and parts of it would go live on the major Scottish and other British networks. Other print and online media would be there too. Police Scotland had their top media people on the case and assured Claire and me that it would be beamed far and wide. Together with what I'd told Claire, the prospective press conference gave her a visible boost. I didn't feel as positive about it myself, but I kept those thoughts private.

I called Douglas as I closed in on the designated pub, but after a few rings it went to voicemail, so I left a brief message and hung up. I cleared my head and focused on the challenge in hand. Even the best plan in the world had its faults, and a reason for it not to work could always be found. The trouble was, I couldn't think of an alternative strategy. The piano teacher had been cleared by the police and I believed their conclusion. I'd vetted him extensively and secretly before Emily's first lesson, and I was convinced that the man was harmless. I did have other enemies, plenty of them too, but I couldn't think of anybody else who would kidnap one of my kids to get to me.

The Falcon was a well-established pub in the Pilton area of Edinburgh. A working-class neighbourhood north of the city centre and close, as far as I knew, to where Cameron Bullard lived. The pub was quite possibly the safest one in town as Bullard frequented it himself, and didn't tolerate any nonsense in a place where he came to relax with his family and close friends. Cameron was a grandfather and a family man. I was pretty sure nothing would happen to me in the pub. It wasn't his style to have violence occur on his home turf. I spotted a parking space and slotted my car in, took a deep breath and got out. A couple of young thugs were hanging around outside, smoking. They straightened themselves up as I approached, but they said nothing. I knew they recognised me, and I noticed one of them throw away his cigarette and slip into the pub before I arrived.

'Here we go!' I thought as I walked past the young hood still outside. He gave me a silent, menacing stare. I smiled as the boy was puffing himself up. Inside me adrenaline was rushing through my veins. I was entering the lion's den, so to speak, and I couldn't help but feel a certain thrill. It was a busy place, young and old having a relaxing Sunday watching football and socialising. My entrance put an obvious damper on the proceedings. Most people in this place could tell when something was about to go down. I kept my hands visible and stood still, assessing my surroundings. It was a fairly big place with a prominent bar running along the back wall. There were tables and seats situated in the front area, with a couple of booths nestled into the short wall on one side, and two doors on the other side. One of these opened into a private area and the other into a corridor where the toilets were located. On the far wall hung a huge flat-screen TV showing a football game. I looked around as the punters scrutinised me.

Aside from the sound of the TV, the place was silent. Then a guy got up from his seat and came towards me. He was a capable-looking guy, his face displaying barely-contained anger. I recognised him as he came closer. It was Mike Law, one of Bullard's main men and the guy who'd called me last Friday. I remembered the brief conversation we'd had, and how it had ended. I found my balance and forced myself to relax. If I had to fight, I would but I also knew that I was completely outnumbered here. It was only in the movies that the hero entered a bar and knocked out half a dozen baddies before leaving, somewhat ruffled, but with his vengeance enforced. If it came to a fight now, I was pretty sure that I would leave on a stretcher! My saving grace was that I couldn't imagine Bullard sanctioning a fight in here. And even thugs like Mike Law knew the importance of respecting Bullard's wishes. Still, I knew I couldn't reveal any weakness; it was the language of prey, and predators killed prey, easy as that. Mike squared himself up in front of me and almost entered my personal space. Close but not quite.

"What do you want?" he asked, his eyes pulsing in fury.

"I need to talk to Mr Cameron Bullard," I replied calmly.

I used Mr as a sign of respect, there wasn't any point in being smart here. Only fools agitate situations when there's no need. I had two main objectives here, the first was to reach out to Bullard and the second was to be able to walk out of here in one piece. Mike was considering my approach and I had to give it to the man, he kept his cool even though he clearly didn't want to.

"Mr Bullard is not here."

I hid my disappointment.

"I understand, can you forward a message to Mr Bullard?"

Mike broke a mean grin and shifted on his feet. His fists were clenched, and I knew he was just itching to go ballistic. I forced myself to stand my ground without appearing ready to tango.

"And what message would you want to forward to Mr Bullard?"

His voice carried a mocking tone – something I ignored.

"Please can he contact me on this number as soon as possible."

I calmly raised my left hand, in which I held a piece of paper containing my new mobile number. Mike considered this for several minutes – or at least that's how it felt to me. I knew he was debating with himself how Bullard would react if he ignored what I'd asked, and instead laid into me. I stood still but inside the adrenaline was pumping fast. I noticed several guys had quietly moved around the room; at least four were located so that they could block my exit. I was confident I could take Mike, but from then on I'd be fighting a losing battle. But I would, nonetheless, fight with rage. I waited. He took the piece of paper out of my hand.

"All right, I will. You'd better leave now."

"Thanks," I said and forced myself to turn.

Was he waiting for me to look away before he launched at me? But nothing happened as I walked out. The guys at the door didn't shift as I squeezed past them. The tension in the pub was at breaking point, but I walked out without anything happening. Outside, a posse of younger guys was hanging around; they stopped talking as I walked past. Nothing was said. I kept it together as I walked slowly back to my car and got in. Once there, I allowed myself to breathe again. I looked back at the pub. The young guys were still staring over at me, but none of them moved. And neither Mike nor anybody else came out of the pub. I started the car and drove away. As I passed by, one of the young guys made a rude gesture towards me, but I just smiled and worked the hands free. Douglas' mobile rang until it went onto voicemail. So much for having my back! I felt annoyed and left an angry message. What on earth was he up to? I didn't dwell on that thought but focused back on what had just happened in the pub. Not much on the surface, but I found it interesting that it had been so civil. Maybe Bullard wasn't involved, and this Jason Stewart guy had been working for somebody else?

"Damn!" I shouted and slapped the steering wheel. I still needed to see Bullard face-to-face. He was suspect number one in my book. I glanced at the clock and saw that I still had some time before I had to collect Claire. My stomach rumbled and reminded me it needed food. I decided to grab something to eat and then head back to my office. First though, I wanted to check on Helena and the kids. I worked the hands free again and after a few rings Helena's lovely voice filled the car.

"Hugo, darling, how's it going?"

She was keeping her voice light, so I knew she was with the kids. They didn't know yet that their oldest sister had been abducted. They were too young to understand – too young to be burdened with this now.

"I'm okay, how's my crew?"

I replied in the same light tone. I could hear the voices of the younger ones in the background. Helena was in the car with the whole lot.

"Daddy, daddy, where are you?" James' happy voice made me smile.

"I'm working, buddy. You and the gang having a great time with mum and Aunty Petite?"

"Right, enough you two! Daddy's busy – he'll join us later," Helena said to James as he started arguing with Ryan about something or other.

It was hard for me to distinguish the finer details of the disagreement over the phone line, but I relished their sweet, innocent voices, and I missed them desperately. I dragged my thoughts back to the here and now.

"Listen Helena – I'll call you later, before the press conference at six."

"Press conference?" Helena asked, and it dawned on me that I hadn't told her.

"Yes, the police think it's a good move, and I agree. I'm going with Claire. I'll call you before it starts," I said, ignoring the slight pang of guilt.

It wasn't as if I'd been larking around. Helena was silent for a moment before she replied. If she felt left out and somewhat ignored, she obviously decided to let it go.

"Right – sounds like a good idea. I assume you and Douglas don't have anything concrete yet then? I'll find somewhere we can watch or listen to that. Let me know which channels it'll be on ... Love you, Hugo."

"I will, love you too."

"Bye ... hey, tell daddy you love him."

Helena encouraged the young ones, and a chorus of "love you" filled my car. I laughed, feeling happy for the first time since news of Emily's abduction had reached me. I said my goodbyes and terminated the call.

ELEVEN

CLAIRE HAD WORKED HARD to build her courage for the forthcoming media event, but as we approached the Fettes Divisional HQ she started to crumble. I reached out and she grabbed my hand. I could feel the tremor coursing through her. We were just a few minutes away and as I glanced over, tears were streaking down her pale face. I didn't know what to say. Her mother leaned forward from the back seat and gently held her shoulder. Claire started to cry, a painful lament from the bottom of her heart. I felt the sweat pop on my brow and struggled to stay calm and in control. I didn't want to cry, but why that was important I didn't know. Maybe I feared that if I gave way to tears now, I wouldn't be able to stop. Ever. Her mother spoke, soothing words that only a mother could provide, but they didn't work. Claire's sobs continued, and they cut right through my heart.

I continued to hold her hand whilst steering with my other one. Driving provided the focus I needed to distant myself from Claire's breakdown. As we approached the police building I noticed several news vans parked outside, a little crowd had assembled near the front door too. They were kept in check by a few uniformed officers. I knew we wanted publicity, that was the whole point of this exercise. But these kinds of events also brought out those who feasted on the misery of others for sheer entertainment. Obviously, most wouldn't admit to such motivation, but hidden behind a façade of concern lurked nothing but raw curiosity. I hated that, I looked at those people and felt nothing but disgust. I was probably projecting my own anger onto them and that worked for me. It was better being angry just now than falling apart in tears. We had a press conference to do and I needed it to go well. Claire could fall apart, but I needed to remain strong and keep her afloat. Perhaps her genuine emotional distress would trigger the necessary remorse or guilt for someone in the know to pick up that phone. A cold analytical way of viewing it, I admit, but whatever worked.

I gently freed my hand from Claire's as I parked the car. She looked over at me, blinked and tried to say something, but then suddenly leaned over and kissed me. Her full lips felt soft on mine. I grabbed her without thinking. I held her until she stopped sobbing, giving her time to pull herself together. Her mother and her two sisters were in the back of the car, silently watching us, tears running down their faces too. I continued to hold Claire, waiting for her breathing to eventually stabilise. I didn't attribute any meaning to the kiss, whatever it was, it was something she just needed to do – there and then.

"You ready, Claire?" I whispered into her mass of hair.

She nodded and then pulled back from me. As she looked around, it seemed that she had only just realised where we were. Eleanor, her oldest sister, leaned forward and laid a hand on her shoulder.

"We're here, Claire. Come on, let's go inside."

I got out of the car and hurried around the vehicle to help Claire. Her mother and sisters filed out and positioned themselves as a human shield against the drama-hungry onlookers. I opened the door and held Claire's hand as she got out. The tremor was still there. She tried to smile. It nearly worked. I smiled back to her and guided her towards the entrance. A couple of reporters were lurking outside and as it dawned on them who we were they rushed in quickly for the kill. Grabbing Claire around the shoulders, I hurried her up the steps. She wasn't up to facing the barrage of questions reporters would surely hurl at her. We got into the police building in one piece and I released Claire from my protective hold. Taking stock of our surroundings, I realised that the reception area was full of media types. Talk about out of the frying pan, into the fire. I should've planned this better, but my mind had been preoccupied. When the media people realised who we were, they turned towards us, and a senior police officer stepped in. I didn't recognise her, but she seemed to be in charge, down here anyway.

"Please, give the family some room. Please respect them. No questions, please."

Her voice carried natural authority, but it had no effect whatsoever: questions exploded from all angles. I caught the police officer's attention as I grabbed Claire's hand. She stumbled in towards me as a wall of people encircled us.

"Right, where do we go?" I barked.

The police officer gestured towards the staircase. I didn't hesitate and pushed away the media types, even those whom I knew to be sympathetic to our cause – it couldn't be helped; I had to protect Claire. She was frozen with fear as the chorus of questions overwhelmed her. Dragging her behind me, I made a dash for the staircase. The senior officer led the way and made a reasonable effort of clearing our path. Still, a few of the media types were physically large and used their bulk to hold their ground. One guy in particular was aggressive; he was a big guy, bearded, with deeply-sunken eyes in a fleshy face. I didn't know which news outfit he represented, but he was right in Claire's face with no concern for her pale, grief-stricken visage. I got up close and looked him straight in the face.

"Back off!" I growled sternly.

He smirked, ignored me and continued to try to get to Claire. I was already hot under the collar, and my anger surged. This guy wasn't going to take heed of 'please'. I allowed people to get close around us and the crowd provided me with the perfect opportunity. I kneed him in a very tender region. He grimaced and buckled forward.

"You okay, mate?" I shouted, faking concern.

Then I broke away and continued to move towards the staircase, pulling Claire along with me. Behind us the big guy keeled over onto the floor, taking a couple of people with him for good measure. One guy shouted, "Cardiac arrest!" and other media types took an immediate interest. Chaos ensued, providing the opportunity we needed to get away.

"Well, I think it's fair to say that could've gone better!"

The senior female officer raised an eyebrow as she commented on the chaos. I cursed silently to myself, really wanting to blame somebody but finding nobody else at fault, other than myself.

"Damned media!" I blurted out.

"Who we need!"

The senior female officer paused for dramatic effect. We looked at each other and I worked hard to swallow the rebuke without snapping back. She was right, obviously. She offered her hand.

"I'm Assistant Chief Constable Gillian Meyer. I'm in charge of media relations at Police Scotland."

I shook her hand and pressed my internal reset button.

"Pleased to meet you. Now what?" I replied a little sheepishly.

"Right, we'll leave this behind us and focus on why we're here. Ms Munro and Mr Storm, come with me, please. We've got to get you guys ready."

She pointed at a door and then headed over.

Claire was still dazed by what had just happened, so I grabbed her hand again and led her with me. Her mother and sisters followed closely. I noticed the Assistant Chief giving them a close look before apparently deciding to let them come too. Just as well, as I knew that they wouldn't readily accept being excluded. They were here for Claire and I knew she needed them. As a family they were close; they fought like cats and dogs at times, but they were there for each other. Thinking of family, my thoughts turned to Douglas. Where exactly was he? As we filed into a seminar room I picked up my mobile and checked the screen. Petite and Helena had called but not Douglas, no text nor missed call.

In the room, four people were sitting on one side of a huge oval conference table. I recognised McGregor and his sidekick; the other two I hadn't seen before. McGregor got up as we filed in and he nodded in acknowledgement to Claire and me.

"Hello, Ms Munro and Mr Storm, please have a seat."

His deep voice rumbled as he gestured to the chairs across from him. The Assistant Chief took a seat at the head of the table. I commandeered the two middle seats for Claire and me, making sure that she was seated before I took my place. Claire was still dazed, her big tearful eyes sought my reassurance. She reached out and grabbed my hand, and I gave hers a little squeeze, together with what I hoped was a strong smile. I could tell she was extremely nervous; inside there was a turmoil of emotions raging. Our worlds had fallen apart only yesterday, that was still very raw. I was playing the strong guy, but inside me too, a hurricane of emotions reigned.

I focused on McGregor opposite, he looked back with deep set hound-dog eyes. I couldn't help but wonder whether he knew what Douglas and I had been up to. I felt like asking him if he knew where Douglas was, but something held me back. As always, when it came to my brother, my instinct told me not to go there.

The Assistant Chief cleared her throat to get our attention. She began with a briefing on what the police operation had discovered so far, and that wasn't much. Woefully little in fact. Whoever had taken Emily was either very lucky, very clever or both. The police had managed to identify what was believed to be the number plate of the van used. That crucial image had been recorded on a fleeting CCTV sequence, six blocks away at a petrol station. It wasn't explicitly stated, but I instantly realised that this was the petrol station adjacent to the supermarket where Claire had been. Emily had most likely been driven past, in the back of this van, whilst her mother was inside that supermarket. Luckily, Claire didn't seem to pick up on that, and I gestured to McGregor hoping he would get my meaning: 'Let's move on and not address that just now'. McGregor took the hint and gently moved the briefing on. The van had subsequently been traced to a builder in Falkirk who'd reported his vehicle stolen that very day. He was totally shocked when the police had turned up with four vehicles and a dozen officers. The police were still questioning him, but were pretty certain that the poor guy wasn't involved. I agreed.

After the briefing the Assistant Chief allowed for questions. Claire and her gang had many, most of which were, understandably, impossible for the police to answer. But I was grateful for the sensitive handling by Meyer and McGregor. I just listened – sometimes it's best just to do that. After a while, Claire and her family were done. With the realisation that nothing new had really been learned, Claire began to cry again, a deep, low lament, full of hurt and helplessness. The police officers sat motionless, and McGregor's face showed no emotion. He had decades of experience of wading through human misery. It did something to one's soul, I understood that. Claire regained her self-control and muttered an apology.

"Don't be sorry, Ms Munro, it's a natural reaction. You're under a lot of stress just now. Don't be too hard on yourself," Meyer said with a compassionate voice.

Claire focussed on her and I saw how hard she worked to pull herself together. I had loved her once, and I realised that part of me still loved her, always would. I was proud of her and I felt a strong sense of protectiveness towards her.

"Thank you, Assistant Chief Meyer. I just want to say how grateful I am for all that you're doing."

Claire's voice was fragile, and each word was heavily laden with her pain. I looked over at the Assistant Chief and nodded my agreement.

Meyer held Claire's eyes and replied, "We're all working on this as best we can. Police Scotland is completely dedicated to this case, I can promise you that."

Some people would've blamed the police for not solving this straight away, and a lot of people would've projected their anger and frustration onto them. The police accepted that. It was normal human behaviour; blame was an instinctive reaction to helplessness, but not for Claire. She was one of the good guys. I knew she couldn't rage against those she knew were trying to find our daughter. It was just the kind of person she was. I admired that.

"Right then, shall we start to prepare for the press conference?"

The Assistant Chief nodded to the appointed person, a media type by the name of Robert Craig and the ordeal began.

The press conference was a bruising event. Afterwards I felt shell shocked. Claire was an even worse wreck than she had been before it started, so I got her out of the room as quickly as possible. I'd never been the main focus of a media event before and neither had Claire. We stumbled out of the room, riddled by cascading emotions of grief, guilt and fear. The sheer focus had been intense and had felt ruthless. Having an image of our little girl as the focus for a dozen or so news outfits really rammed the message home. This wasn't a nightmare; it was real – very real. I held on to Claire as she sobbed her heart out. Would her tears ever end? Her mother and sisters followed closely behind. Once outside they intervened and took control.

"We'll take Claire to a quiet room I think, Hugo ... don't you agree?" Eleanor looked directly at me, her voice was cracking up and all colour had drained from her face, but she was just about holding it together.

"Uh ... yes, probably a good idea," I agreed, looking at Claire whilst wondering if she'd ever recover.

A police officer gestured for them to enter a room. A safe zone, I presumed, where they could process, in protected privacy, what they'd been through. The officer invited me in too, but I declined. More than anything, I wanted to get out there again, hunting. I knew I couldn't sit in a room, dwelling on the problem – I needed to keep moving. If I sat still now, I feared I would fall apart. A hand landed on my shoulder and I spun around quickly.

"Oh, take it easy, Hugo."

It was McGregor. I stood looking at him for a moment, aware that we were being watched. I controlled my breathing and the rage that was building inside of me.

"Sorry McGregor, just a little edgy I guess," I mumbled.

"Don't be sorry. I just wanted to say you guys did terrific."

McGregor's sleepy eyes drilled through mine – seeking information maybe? I shook my head, forcing away the paranoia.

"Thanks, now what?"

"Well, now we man the phones and see what comes in. There will be calls – maybe one of them will give us what we need."

He paused and scratched his fleshy chin, obviously considering his next step. I decided to move this on. I didn't want him to ask me any questions about Douglas.

"Okay, can I ask you to take Claire and her family home? I'm hitting the streets again. And if anything crucial comes in, you will contact me straight away – yes?" I was itching to get going.

"Yes, we'll take them home. And yes, we'll contact you straight away ... by the way, do you know where Douglas is?"

He threw out that last part in an off-hand manner, as if it was an after-thought, but I didn't believe that for a moment.

"Great. And, sorry, I don't know where Douglas is," I replied simply.

I didn't want to expand on this with McGregor, but I was intrigued; where on earth was he? I had no idea.

"Right then, take care out there, Hugo."

McGregor's low voice made me wonder whether he meant something more than he was saying. My mind felt numb.

"Thanks. Please tell Claire I'll call her later, but tell her not stay up for the call."

I waited for McGregor to confirm this and then I left, successfully dodging the last few reporters as I exited the building. As I drove off, I let out a sigh of relief.

Working the hands free again, I called Douglas, but once more the call went straight to voice mail. I cursed and wondered whether to call his wife. She was an ice queen, a stuck-up bitch from a very wealthy family who didn't approve of Douglas and his successful courtship of a potential fat inheritance pot. To be fair, Douglas was an obvious gold digger. Mary wasn't my type, even when she was young, before the bitterness had completely poisoned her, but I remember how excited Douglas had been about her family wealth when they were dating. Helena and I had agreed that Mary had married Douglas just to annoy her family. It was fair to say that she had succeeded. But then she found out that the joke was on her; she was the one stuck with Douglas. The romance ended quickly, and she soon began to dislike him intensely, even hating the man according to Helena. Why she didn't divorce him, I never understood. Maybe she was still proving a point? Anyway, Douglas wasn't home a lot, almost never I guessed. But could he be home just now?

Mary Storm-Witheringham, the stuck-up bitch, had ostentatiously hyphenated her maiden name with Douglas' surname. She was a double-barrelled snob. She didn't like me either. It was mutual disgust. Would she even tell me if Douglas was home? I hadn't heard from her since Emily had disappeared and she would've known about that. Mean, unnatural woman. I couldn't remember the last time I'd spoken to her. I cursed and worked the screen. There was only one way of finding out. Douglas' home number was there somewhere. Just as I found the number, a black Ranger Rover Sport cut in front of me and forced me to do an emergency stop. I cursed loudly as my Audi came to a halt with what seemed like only an inch to spare. Then I noticed a similar Ranger Rover stopped behind me. I was boxed in, and deliberately so. I briefly considered ramming myself free, my Audi was a powerful, heavy car but still the two Range Rovers were heavier. A guy got out of the Ranger Rover in front and came over towards my driver-side window. He was dressed in a black suit and holding something up in his right hand for me to see. I focused and quickly realised it was a pistol, it looked like a Glock. I wasn't armed, so there wasn't anything I could do. But he was holding the pistol up for me to see, he wasn't pointing it at me. I recognised him – it was Mike Law. As he approached my side window, he indicated for me to lower it. I did as the man asked. If he was to shoot me, the glass window wouldn't help. He quickly scanned the inside of the car.

"Keep your hands where I can see them, Hugo."

"What's going on, Mike!" I spoke calmly whilst my keeping my cool.

"Mr Bullard wants to see you. He got your message. But he wants a face-to-face meeting." Mike looked up as a car approached us from behind. He took a step back and shielded the gun. The step back was a smart move, just making sure I couldn't easily grab him whilst he was distracted. Not that I was going to do anything stupid anyway, I wanted to talk to Bullard.

TWELVE

I FOLLOWED MIKE'S RANGER Rover through Edinburgh, he had refused to tell me where we were heading. I wasn't much of a poker player, my gambling debt proved that, but I had promised myself that whenever I had a losing hand, I would act accordingly. Mike was driving sensibly and making it easy for me to follow him, but the drive, together with the fatigue, was starting to make my eyes sting. Boy, was I tired. I blasted the cabin with a cool breeze through the air con in an attempt to keep my mind sharp. The adrenaline would return when we arrived at our destination. Outside, the miserable weather continued, the gloom was all encompassing. As we headed up the bypass, a call jolted me out of a slowly-descending sleepiness. I pressed the hands-free button on the steering wheel and Helena's worried voice filled the cabin.

"Hugo, you okay?"

"Hi darling. Yeah, I'm fine, what's up?"

"I saw the press conference on the TV ... so sad. Terrible ..." Helena's voice ran out of steam.

She wanted to talk, understandably, but I had neither time nor energy to deal with that just now. However, I didn't want to hurt her feelings. The leading car was indicating to exit the bypass at the junction that I would normally take to go home. That made me sit up and take notice. We were heading in the direction of my home, a fact which certainly cleared my head fast and brought me back to my senses.

"It was ... Listen Helena, I'm involved in something just now."

"I see, you will be safe, yes?"

Her voice was a mix of worry and disappointment, but I couldn't do anything about it there and then.

"Yes. I'm fine, but I've got to go, okay? I'll call you later," I lied, and followed the Range Rover onto the ramp and off the motorway.

"Okay. Oh, before you go – Petite just told me somebody has contacted her – Kim Monteith – she says she needs to talk to you," Helena's voice suddenly had an energy to it.

"What, Kim Monteith?"

I checked that I'd heard her correctly. That was Ariella's business manager. Why did she want to talk to me?

"Yes, that's what Petite told me. That's important, isn't it? You want to speak to her?" Helena's voice was keen, and I knew she wanted me to speak to Petite right away, but I couldn't, not just now. The drowsiness had lifted, and my mind was racing. I had no idea why Ariella's business manager would contact me directly at this time. But somehow, I knew it had to be important. However, Mike was still heading towards my neighbourhood. Things suddenly seemed to be heating up.

"Listen Helena, tell Petite I'll call her as soon as I can, but I've got to go now. Love you."

I terminated the call as the Ranger Rover turned into my street, and a cold shiver ran down my spine; my street was a dead end. I'd lived in this street for a good number of years, and neither Cameron Bullard nor any of his associates lived here. We were heading towards my home. I hadn't expected this. Potential scenarios were rushing through my brain. I was fully amped up and ready to unleash. Was Emily here? Tied up and held by one of Bullard's thugs? Was this it? I knew if he'd caused her any harm, I would go ballistic and attack them all, regardless of numbers. I also knew I had to restraint myself and keep my cool to save Emily. Otherwise we were both dead. They would know that I'd go crazy, and Bullard would have taken that into account. The man was ruthless, and very smart.

Mike's Ranger Rover came to a halt in front of my house, and Mike jumped out quickly. This time the gun was pointed directly at me as he approached. Trees shaded us from my neighbours. It was a quiet street anyway, with all the houses located well away from the road. I kept my hands visible and waited until he came up to my window. My heart was pounding in my chest, but under control. My senses were all intensely focused. I couldn't mess this up. Mike gestured for me to get out of the car. I did so calmly, whilst keeping my hands clearly visible. My eyes flashed fury, but I kept my mouth shut. Threats were pointless. I noticed two cars parked in my drive. Two big black Mercedes saloons. It was an indication of Bullard's confidence, that he'd parked right there on my drive. Mike got my attention back.

"Okay, you're keeping your cool. Good. Mr Bullard is waiting for you inside your house. We'll go inside now, without any drama – and there'll be no drama when we get inside! You understand?"

"No drama. Let's go!"

I spoke through gritted teeth. My rage was at boiling point, but giving way to it would've been a fatal mistake. Mike wouldn't hesitate to gun me down. I noticed the pistol had a silencer attached. He took a step back, gesturing to two other goons to get out of the Ranger Rover. They too were dressed in black suits. My neighbours all knew of my unorthodox business; seeing these characters with me outside my house would spark curiosity, but not alarm.

"You're a cool customer, Hugo, I'll give you that. Now follow Chris."

Mike smiled, as this huge guy, Chris, headed to my front door and I followed. He was enjoying this. I might have looked cool on the outside, but on the inside I was in utter turmoil. This was my home, where my wife and my young kids lived, but now a ruthless gangster boss was waiting for me inside, perhaps with my oldest child, who'd been snatched yesterday. I continued to keep my cool. Behind me Mike and the other goon followed. The big guy opened the door and walked straight in, noting that the door was undamaged. So much for the locks and security system I'd installed. I knew Helena would've locked and armed the security when she left yesterday.

"Mr Bullard is waiting for you in the living room," Mike said as he followed me inside.

I didn't reply, but just headed in that direction. True, it was my house but it felt strange, as if its whole character had changed. I could hear the TV was on as I opened the glass door. Stepping in, I saw Bullard sitting in my comfortable recliner chair watching BBC News on my wall-mounted flat screen. I stopped and nervously looked around.

"You looking for your daughter?" Bullard asked as he lowered the volume on the TV.

My heart ticked up a further notch. The turmoil inside threatened to flatten me. I forced myself to keep calm.

"Where is she?" I asked in a low, intense voice as I scanned the room.

Two huge guys were standing either side of Bullard. One of them looked rough, with a busted lip and a swollen right eye. I focused back on Bullard, and as I met his dark eyes, my desire to attack him intensified, making me feel dizzy.

"Not here!" Bullard replied, matter of fact.

His face remained neutral, as he took a sip from one of my coffee cups.

"Don't mess with me, Bullard. Where's Emily?"

"I'm not messing with you – not like you thought you could mess with me."

His voice was angry now and his eyes radiated rage. I took a step forward, clenching my fists, the two thugs stepped forward too.

"I'll fix that, but you've got to give me back my daughter," I said.

My words sounded so lame but he had me by the throat. Mike was behind me with his gun aimed at my back. I forced myself to stop before this got out of hand.

"I would if I could, but I can't," Bullard paused and took another sip of the coffee. He nodded his approval and lifted the cup up towards me.

"Your coffee machine is quite decent! Anyway, I don't have your daughter."

A tense silence lingered as I tried to digest what he was saying.

"What do you mean? What on earth is this?" My head was now spinning.

"I didn't kidnap your daughter, you stupid fool!" Bullard snapped, leaning forward.

I just looked at him, certain that my legs would go at any moment. My gut instinct told me that he was telling the truth.

"You really think I would take a little girl to get to you?" His words conveyed his anger loud and clear. Then he leaned back, shaking his head before continuing, "Damn, Hugo! It's a good thing I like you," he chuckled, adding, "You've crossed way over the line, Hugo. Mike here wanted me to put the screws on you, and I had decided to do just that. But then this tragedy happened. Now, what the hell should I do about you?"

"Can I sit?" I asked lamely. I felt as deflated as a spent balloon.

"Yeah, sure. It's your house!"

Bullard chuckled again to himself. His thugs laughed with him; that was the politically correct thing to do, I guessed. Even the guy with the busted lip and swollen eye seemed to find it funny, until I gave him a hard stare. He stepped further towards me, his fists ready, and I noticed he was wearing a knuckle duster covered in blood.

"Hey, stand down Mitch," Bullard ordered sternly and looked over at me as I took a seat on the sofa.

"Mitch here lost his good looks because of your maverick brother."

I looked up quickly.

"Douglas! What has happened to Douglas?"

"We had a talk, you might say. Douglas let us in, you see, but not willingly. I had to threaten to shop him in to his employer, and threaten your Helena for good measure before he let us in." Bullard paused and broke a mean grin before continuing, "Sure didn't care what I said I'd do to his dear wife though. Shocking. You Storm brothers are something else. Anyway, we had a talk. I had to use some hard-boiled tactics. Still the hard-head wouldn't talk. See, I like you, Hugo, but I am not that keen on your brother. He took out two of my men, and Mitch here took some hurt too."

"Where is he?" I asked quickly.

"Sleeping!" Bullard said, and lifted an eyebrow.

'Sleeping!' I wondered what he meant.

Bullard read my thoughts, "Relax, he's still alive. Now, I've got to ask you a couple of questions."

I leaned forward and looked him straight in the eyes.

"Okay, what?"

"See, my useless nephew, Jack, is missing. The boy is an idiot but still he's family. You wouldn't know anything about that, would you?"

Bullard looked at me intensely. Sometimes in life you stand on the edge of a cliff, and even the smallest touch is enough to push you over the edge. I concentrated hard on keeping my face neutral and shook my head – not too vigorous though, just enough to convey my innocence, I hoped. And then I answered in a voice that successfully masked the internal turmoil.

"No, sorry, don't have a clue. I've been busy, Mr Bullard!"

Bullard just sat there staring at me. I knew he was deciding whether he was going to believe me or not. I managed to return his stare as he pondered further before putting down his cup and grasping his fingers together.

"Right, Douglas denied any knowledge too, even after Mitch here took off one of his fingers." He paused to gauge my reaction, but I didn't respond, so he continued, "See, there's a problem here. There's a rumour going around that Jason Stewart had arranged to meet this dirty drug cop yesterday; he's not been seen since. Jason is another idiot, but he's close with Jack. This dirty cop sounds awfully like your brother."

"I'm telling you, Mr Bullard, I don't know anything about any Jason, or your nephew."

I lied with true conviction. That's the way to lie, make it so you believe it yourself. And don't spin on it, say as little as possible; talking only digs you deeper into a hole.

Another silence ensued, as Bullard evaluated me and my story. I waited – nothing else for it. These guys were good at what they did. There were plenty of stupid criminals, but Bullard made sure that those close to him were the smarter ones. Bullard let out a sigh, and got up. Then he looked at me and laughed, beckoning me over.

"What am I supposed to do with you, Hugo? Come here."

He held his arms out. I got up and went over, unsure but nonetheless doing as I'd been told. Just as I moved in for a hug with the devil, the big guy on my right caught me off guard, preventing me from noticing the other on my left. Too late I realised I was being tasered. The pain was sharp, all-encompassing and severe. My head felt like it had exploded. I was out for the count as I went down.

THIRTEEN

I AWOKE WITH A SPLITTING headache, my whole body racked with pain. I tried to lift my head, but it felt like a concrete block. Cautiously, I lowered it again, and gave myself a few minutes to recover. My mind was slowly resurfacing from the abyss. Somebody had put me into the recovery position. I realised I was lying on my living room floor. Fragments of what had happened started to filter through, just like the sunlight, as it beamed through the large window. Slowly I moved into a sitting position. It took a great effort, and I grunted with pain as I forced myself to get up. The room started to spin as I stood, and I reached out for the chair, falling into it. I sat back and waited for the spinning to slow down. When I was confident that it had, I looked around the room; it looked like it did every other day. I remembered the TV had been on, now it was off. The house was quiet but, outside, bird song could be heard. I focused on my wristwatch, it was just before five o'clock in the morning. I gently rotated my shoulders and head, trying to loosen up. My neck felt awfully stiff. A burning pain made its presence felt on my left flank. Taser – I recalled that the thugs had tasered me. Were they still here? I couldn't hear anything, other than my own breathing and groaning; the house was dead quiet.

So, it wasn't Bullard – I believed him. If it had been done for revenge he would've said so, and if it had a particular purpose he would have laid that out too. The man was ruthless, but he had a code. Somebody else had taken Emily, I was sure of that. Thoughts of Emily made me ignore my pain and get up. I still felt a little dizzy, but I wouldn't let that hold me back. I noticed an envelope on the coffee table, and saw that it was addressed to me. Filled with trepidation, I picked it up and opened it. Inside was a sheet of white A4 paper, containing a neatly handwritten note:

'Hugo, you've got one week to get me the money, otherwise I will take your house. Now go and get your daughter.'

I re-read the message several times, just to be certain. Bullard was giving me a week's grace! I knew I was very lucky; the man must, for whatever reason, really like me to have given me that concession. Thinking of that made me remember Douglas – where on earth was he? He had been here, forced to allow access to Bullard and his crew. Was he still here? Was he dead? I looked around – no Douglas lying in my living room. I folded the note and slipped it into my pocket. Bullard had said he wasn't keen on my brother. No surprise there, not many people did like Douglas. That didn't bode well for Douglas. I took a deep breath and started to search downstairs. Entering the kitchen I stopped suddenly, seeing the splattered blood, not only on the floor but also up the walls. The room was a total mess. The heavy kitchen table, together with a couple of chairs were broken. I could just imagine the scene: cornered in here, Douglas would've fought like a wounded lion. But this time, he had lost, outnumbered. A chill ran down my spine as I remembered that one of his fingers had been clipped off. What had happened to the rest of the man? I knew I had to check outside and in the garage, but as I looked around the house I became more and more certain that Bullard had taken Douglas away with him, dead or alive. If he was dead, I doubted that I'd ever find him again. Bullard took extreme care in making dead bodies disappear, a dead person led to more trouble than a missing person. And considering Douglas' shady life-style, the notion that he would've packed up and disappeared was more than believable. I stood for a moment, looking at the mess. Helena and the kids couldn't come home and see this. She would leave with the kids and never return. I needed to clean it up. I could explain the damaged furniture; maybe Douglas and I had had a fight? Helena would believe that, but blood splattered up the walls and everywhere, no way. I rolled up my sleeves and got to work. Within the hour I'd cleaned it up pretty well. Then I searched the rest of the house to make sure I hadn't overlooked any blood stains. In my home office there was another mess, but no blood. My mobile phone was on my desk, but I couldn't recall how it had got there. Bullard must've taken it off me after I went down. I had enhanced security on my phone and nobody knew the passwords. I didn't trust fingerprint identity; if you were unconscious, using one of your fingers was easy enough for someone else to do. So, I was pretty sure Bullard hadn't managed to browse through it.

I quickly tidied up the mess in there, sat down behind my desk and worked the security sequence. I noticed several missed calls from Helena and Petite as well as one from a number I didn't recognise. Then it dawned on me: Helena had told me yesterday that Kim Monteith, Ariella's business manager, needed to speak to me. I called Helena. Her voice told me she was in a very stressed state as she had repeatedly tried to contact me without success, and nobody else knew where I was. A certain fear had taken hold of her and I had to talk her out of it. She cried, so I continued to reassure her that I'd just been very busy and that I was fine. I somehow managed to keep the pain out of my voice. I left out what had actually happened. Nothing good would come from her knowing about that. After I was sure that she'd calmed down, I asked to speak to Petite.

"You okay, Hugo?" Petite's voice came on the line.

"Listen, are the kids there with Helena?"

"They are now."

"Good, use that as an excuse, and go for a walk alone. I'll wait."

"I hear you." I heard the low voices of Petite and Helena talking, then Petite walking. I waited for her to find an appropriate place. After a few minutes she came back on the line.

"You alone now?" I checked.

"Yes, I'm sitting in the car."

"Tell me about this Kim Monteith."

"Right, she called late last night. She said she'd only give the information to you, and only when she was safe. And she insisted you mustn't contact Ariella, any of her family or other associates, and if they contact you, then you should not mention anything to them about speaking to her. If you do, she will simply disappear and whatever she wanted to tell you will go with her. She seemed genuine, but very scared."

I took a moment to digest what I was being told here. This was very significant, I felt certain of that. The lead I thought I had with Bullard was dead, but now suddenly I had something else to go on. I felt a rush of excitement as ideas raced around my mind. If the information Kim had was about Chloe, Ariella's daughter, then why wouldn't she just talk directly to Ariella? It was obvious that she didn't trust Ariella or those around her. I tried hard to clear my head, I needed to take each step with care.

"How did she get your number?"

"She wouldn't say, but we've moved location since she first called me. I was sure we hadn't been followed. Even so, I'll ditch this mobile after this conversation and we'll move again. The kids are getting tired of the disruption, but we're still managing to make it fun."

"Thank you, Petite, I can't tell you how grateful I am."

"No problem, Hugo. You thinking the same as me, yes? This has got to be linked to Emily!"

I nodded – yeah – I sure was thinking the same.

"Yes indeed! Did she say how I was to contact her?"

"She left a mobile number. Different one from the one she called on. I guess she's using multiple phones here. She's undoubtedly living in fear, but she's still keeping up appearances, from what I can tell."

"Give it to me," I requested. Petite read out the number and I repeated it, committing it to memory.

"Great. Thank you again, Petite. Now, tell Helena I'm following up this call from this woman. You guys move again, and I'll contact you as soon as I can. Send me a text in a couple of hours with your new number, make it a sale feedback enquiry."

"Got it, Hugo. You going to change mobiles before you call her?"

"Yes, for good measure. Speak soon." I terminated the call. My house had been compromised, maybe my mobile had too. I'd been a little too confident about the security of my phone. Even the best security could be hacked. I needed a new mobile and a fresh number. I decided not to trust the ones I had in the house. Instead I decided to go to a shop and buy a cheap phone and a pay-as-you-go SIM. Right now, paranoia was a good tactic. My mobile blipped just as I was about to get up, and I saw an email – another from Ariella. It was short and to the point:

'Dear Hugo, please contact me as soon as possible. I saw the press conference yesterday, and feel utterly devastated for you. Your sincerely, Ariella Cantor.'

I sat for a moment, looking at the email. In the end I decided not to trust this lady, at least not until I'd spoken to Kim. I replied with a brief message:

'Dear Ms Cantor, thank you for your email. I will contact you soon. Take care.

Yours sincerely, Hugo Storm.'

Then I got up and went for a quick shower. Nothing seemed to have been touched upstairs; toys littered the bedrooms, and everything was as I reckoned it would've been when Helena and the kids had left. But I knew Bullard and his men had been here. I wondered whether we would ever be able to live here again as a family, as I picked out a fresh set of clothes and turned the shower on. The taser had left marks on my flank, and my skin burned fiercely as the water washed over it. Still the shower made me feel almost human again. Almost. I dressed quickly and checked the hidden safe. It appeared to be intact. Inside, the contents were the same as the last time I had checked. It appeared that Bullard and the crew had missed that one. I left the house and glanced over at the garage when a thought struck me like a bolt of lightning. Douglas! Was he in there? I had completely forgotten to check the garage! I didn't believe he would be there, but I had to look. To my relief, there was no dead Douglas to be seen, so I headed over to my car, which was parked at the curb where I'd left it. I took out a scanner that I'd picked up from the garage, and used it on the car. No transmitter seemed to be attached, but there were some very advanced tracking devices out there. I decided I needed a fresh car as well, but for now I would have to use this one. I got in and drove off.

Twenty minutes later I locked the car at a park-and-ride outside the city, and jumped onto a shuttle bus heading for Edinburgh centre. I used the first part of the ride to discreetly study my fellow passengers. Nobody triggered suspicion; I was pretty sure I hadn't been followed. Still I was going to proceed with caution. My thoughts wandered back to Douglas and I called his mobile. Again, it went straight onto voicemail. Putting my phone away, I wondered if I would ever see him again. I knew I had to block those thoughts just now. Running through dreadful scenarios wouldn't do me any favours. Douglas would have to wait; I would deal with whatever had happened to him later. Emily was more urgent and required my complete concentration. I cleared my head and focused on the city landscape as the bus was driving ever nearer the centre. Edinburgh, my town, a city I loved – and now hated – was still the place I considered as home. Even though my father was Norwegian, and Norway was dear to my heart, Edinburgh was the place where I had grown up. When I was with Claire, and Emily was young, we had briefly discussed the possibility of moving to Norway, but we never got as far as doing it.

A sudden stop by the bus jolted me out of my deep thoughts. I looked around and realised we were in the city centre, I pressed the stop button and got up. Princess Street was heaving, people everywhere, and it was a nice day, with a blue sky and warm for the time of year. People were smiling and enjoying themselves as they weaved in and out of the never-ending throng of window shoppers. After satisfying myself that the others, who had got off the bus at the same stop, had no interest in me, I headed for the nearest mobile phone shop. The keen salesperson tried gamely to get me to buy one of the more expensive mobiles. I resisted his sales patter, and picked a cheap one along with a pay-as-you-go SIM. I paid in cash, gave the hard-selling chap a fake email address, and left promptly. Out on the street, I decided to visit the establishment of a good friend, and call this Kim person from there.

As usual, Charlie Thomson was behind the bar at his fine establishment, The Tap, just off George Street. The Tap wasn't big but was regularly busy, a place where business people of the shady sort would come and talk shop. Charlie was involved in lots of deals, some were sealed with a handshake over the bar, others, the shadier ones, were concluded in his back office. As I stepped in, I saw Charlie leaning over the bar deep in conversation with a couple of banker types, the sleazy sort, no doubt hacking out another sleaze-ball investment venture over a fine malt. Charlie was ten years my senior and already had silver grey hair. Like Richard Gere he hadn't fought it, he'd embraced it. He was a stylish man who liked to look good. The bar fell silent as the punters noticed me. Charlie looked over, and his face flashed a look of surprise before he excused himself and came over to greet me.

"Hugo Storm! Well I never! Just a minute," he said, and turned to the younger fellow who worked behind the bar with him. "Tam, take the bar, will you?" Tam, a rake-thin, tall guy dressed in black, looked to me like a guy who spent as much time in front of a mirror as did most young women. Kids nowadays!

I walked through the bar, nodding and shaking hands with the guys. I already knew most of them. They all offered their concerned thoughts about Emily. I'd done jobs for many of them. Most I liked, some I couldn't stand. Charlie got out from behind the bar, opened the door to his back office and waved me in. I stepped inside, and he closed the door behind us. We shook hands and embraced in a bear hug.

"Have a seat, Hugo. I've heard your news, of course. I'm so sorry. Can I do anything to help?" Charlie's tone was sympathetic. We both sat down.

"Thanks, Charlie. Listen, I need to make a phone call in private, and then I wondered if I could borrow your car?"

"Of course, it's parked outside, I'll get you the keys – I guess you're in a hurry?"

"Yes, I'll fill you in, but not just now. Is that okay?"

"Of course, my friend. You got a lead, yes?" He leaned forward, his intelligent eyes full of sympathy. Charlie knew Emily too, and always made an effort on her birthdays and at Christmas.

"Yeah, I think I have ..." I paused and thought for a second before continuing. "You haven't heard from Douglas, have you?"

Charlie shook his head and replied, "No, not since last Friday when he was trying to get hold of you. He was worked up about something!" His last words hung there as an invitation for me to grab. I ignored it.

"Sorry for being abrupt here, but is it okay if I have some privacy now?"

"Yes, certainly, I'll leave you to it, just let me get the keys. Listen, and I mean this, if there's anything I can do, you must not hesitate to ask. Anything, Hugo!" Charlie got up to leave, having given me his firm assurance of unreserved assistance.

"I appreciate that, Charlie and I will get back to you, I promise."

Charlie smiled and went over to his desk, unlocked the drawers and pulled out a key. As he came over he dropped it into my hand. He hesitated for a moment. I knew he wasn't offended that I'd cut him short; Charlie always had perspective, he knew this was important.

"I'll be outside. You want a coffee, something to eat?"

"I'm fine thanks, just let me do this, and I'll grab a coffee afterwards."

"You bet, take your time," Charlie said, and touched my shoulder before he walked out. As the door closed behind him, I quickly got the mobile working. I took a deep breath and let it out slowly. Here we go. The number rang seven times before a sensual voice answered.

"Hello, who is this?"

"This is Hugo Storm, may I speak to Kim Monteith please?" I held my breath whilst the person hesitated. I guess, she was making up her mind about taking the plunge.

"Speaking. Thank you for returning my call, Mr Storm."

I almost shouted out in triumph but controlled myself. I tightly clenched my right fist.

"Not a problem. You spoke to my assistant, Ms Williams, earlier. She told me you had information for me. Can I ask to whom this information relates?"

Another pause, another moment of anxious breathing followed. I waited.

"Not so fast, Mr Storm. We need to meet. But I can tell you that it is related to your present situation."

I shot up from the chair and started pacing the office. I could sense how nervous she was, and I knew if I pressed too hard she would hang up. I swallowed hard. She had information about Emily, it had to be important, it had to be crucial, this lady wasn't tricking me, her tense voice told me so.

"Okay, I'm sorry for being forward here. We need to meet. Please tell me what you want me to do?"

She hadn't asked whether I'd spoken to anybody else, she would assume if I had done so, I would lie about it anyway and say that I hadn't. She was obviously nervous but nevertheless she seemed very professional.

"I need you to come to a meeting point. When I am satisfied you are alone I will give you another meeting point. Can you do that?"

"Yes. Tell me where to go." I didn't hesitate. I had Charlie's car key in my other hand.

"Helix Park, outside Falkirk. Go there and sit beside the horse head that bows. I will contact you again then."

"Got it!" I said as the call was terminated. I looked at the mobile screen. Depending on traffic it would take me about forty-five minutes to get there. I had been there once with Helena and the kids, including Emily. The Park was near to Falkirk Football Stadium and close to the M9 motorway. I worked the screen again and fired off a brief message to Petite: 'Contact made – meeting arranged.' I didn't wait for a reply, but left the office and dashed past the bar. I saw Charlie and gestured to say I'd call him. He nodded, and with a serious face flipped his thumb up.

His car was parked, just as he had said, outside. Charlie was a Jaguar man, as long as I'd known the man he'd driven the 'cats'. Business must've been going well because his latest sledge was a top-of-the-range XJ supercharged saloon. I got in and fired up the engine. The cat awoke, and I drove off. It was tempting to hammer it, but I restrained myself. I didn't have time to be stopped by the police, not now. Still there's a difference between speeding and driving efficiently. I got through Edinburgh fast, traffic for a change was on my side. The M9 was a lovely road, and if you knew it well, it was easy to predict where potential police interceptors might be. The Jaguar stretched its legs and I drove fast towards the park. I felt hopeful yet nervous as this could be a make-or-break point. The chance of finding my girl seemed more real than at any time since she had disappeared.

The park was always popular with families as it had several kids' features. However, it was a Monday, a school day, so I didn't have a problem finding a parking space. I slotted the Jaguar into a free bay and got out. Within ten minutes I was at the famous, huge, metal horse heads that dominated the park. I wandered around, looking at the people around me. It was busier than I thought it would be, and the weather had turned a little. It wasn't raining but the wind had made people put their jackets on and hoods up. I found the bench where I assumed Ms Monteith wanted me to sit, and duly sat down. I took out the mobile and stared at it, trying to will it to ring. Nothing. Minutes passed but she didn't call. I forced myself to remain seated. It was extremely hard, but I had to – I'd got here speedily, probably faster than she'd calculated. And she was probably looking at me right now, making sure I was alone. I looked around and saw a few solitary people further away, but I didn't know what she looked like. There were a couple of individuals walking around at a distance, who looked like women, and I realised that it would've been possible for them to have observed me from different angles. But was Ms Monteith alone? Perhaps she had a bodyguard with her, so maybe they were one of the couples who were looking at me just now? There were several of those. Frustration replaced my initial optimism and I stared at the mobile again. I considered calling her, but that wasn't the instruction, and I knew I had to stick to the rules that she'd laid down, otherwise she would disappear. Twenty minutes passed. Just as I was about to lose my patience the mobile rang. I looked at the screen, a withheld number was calling. I forced myself to answer calmly.

"Good, you are here. Now, there is a plastic folder stuck underneath the bench. Open it and follow the instructions within," Ms Monteith said, ending the call before I could say anything.

I looked at the mobile in frustration. This James Bond stuff felt a little over the top. But maybe it wasn't: she had to be fearful for her life. I bent down and searched with my hand under the bench, and sure enough a small plastic folder was stuck there. I brought it out and opened it. Inside a note told me the following. 'Go to Central Valley Hospital – further up the M9 – go in through the front entrance and turn left up to the restaurant – buy two coffees – find a table and wait. Bring this note with you.'

FOURTEEN

I SAT BACK, A HOSPITAL, one place I hadn't considered but which made sense. I assumed this was a large regional hospital, a busy place with people of all sorts coming and going. It was a good setting for observing somebody from a distance, and then approaching when safe. This Kim was obviously smart, but that was only to be expected, since she worked for Ariella Cantor, and only people of the highest calibre lasted in her employment. I folded the note and walked back to the car whilst trying to guess who of all the people around me could possibly be Kim. None stood out. Back in the car I checked my mobile and noticed a message from a new number. It was Petite, she needed me to contact her urgently. Petite was the coolest operator I had ever known and that included the guys who I'd served with in Army Intelligence. If she said urgent, you didn't delay. I rang her mobile whilst tapping the wheel. Things were happening fast, I needed to keep a level head here.

"Hugo, you alone?" Petite didn't waste any time on niceties.

"Yes, what's up?"

I steeled myself for bad news. Just as long it didn't involve Helena and the little ones or some horrific news about Emily; I could cope with everything else.

"One of my police contacts has just informed me that an arrest warrant has been issued for Douglas, and Inspector McGregor is trying to get hold of you. Apparently, the man is not happy." She stopped, giving me the chance to digest her words.

"What the hell, what's the arrest warrant for?"

"My police contact can't say. McGregor is involved but they're keeping it tight. Police Scotland are convinced Douglas – and you – have inside information," she laughed before continuing, "Guess they're right on that one."

I didn't find it particularly funny.

"Any indication I might be next for an arrest warrant?"

I knew this was a loaded question; my enquiry implied that I'd been up to no good, but Petite didn't dig. She knew I'd been searching for Emily without consideration for what I could and couldn't do within a legal context.

"No, but McGregor is trying to reach you. Apparently, the man is frustrated. Probably not helping that they can't find Douglas either."

She paused as she considered what to say next. I didn't hurry her; I was busy trying to prioritise this, versus what I was already involved in.

"Do you know where Douglas is?" Petite asked.

"No, I haven't seen him since yesterday afternoon, but I know that yesterday evening he was in the claws of Cameron Bullard."

I paused and checked the time – I didn't have time for this – I needed to cut it short.

"Listen, I've got to go, I'm following instructions to meet up with Kim. I can't deal with Douglas just now. But can you spread the word and see if anybody knows anything?"

"Sure, will do, Hugo. You okay, you need back up?"

"No, I'm fine. But do me a favour, Petite: call McGregor and tell him I can't contact him just now as I'm hot on the trail of a promising lead."

I'd been mulling that idea over for the last few minutes. There were risks involved, but McGregor needed to know a little; soon I might be needing him a lot.

"You sure, Hugo? McGregor's going to want more, a lot more."

"Yeah, I know, but you just profess ignorance, which is true. You really don't know where I am or what I'm doing. I might be needing Police Scotland later today – I hope so actually."

"I understand. I'll call him, and then what should I do?"

"Don't call me, I'll call you. I am going off grid, so to speak. And please reassure Helena."

"You take care, Hugo. I'll speak to some people about Douglas, handle the police and take care of Helena and the kids. Not a problem."

"Thank you. Have you been told recently that you're awesome?"

I smiled to myself as I posed that question. Petite was indeed awesome, I couldn't have managed without her.

"A couple of times, but thank you, Boss. Now go!" She laughed and terminated the call.

I dropped the mobile and drove off. It took less than ten minutes to reach the Central Valley Hospital, a sprawling building, pig ugly, but modern. I found a parking space and got out.

The restaurant was big and getting busy. I bought the coffees and secured a table next to the large windows. Then I waited, sipped my coffee and people-watched. There was the normal mix of staff, patients and visitors. Nobody seemed interested in me though. After another half an hour or so, a lady doctor arose from a table further in and approached me. She wore a stethoscope around her neck and an agency badge was clipped to her blouse. I couldn't help but smile as Kim Monteith sat down opposite me. I was duly impressed; this lady was smart. She was also good-looking, tall and fit, having the same Mediterranean tan and look as Ariella. I wondered if she was Jewish too.

"Hugo Storm, I presume?" she said and flashed her dazzlingly white teeth.

"Yes, and you are Kim Monteith. Nice to meet you, doctor."

Kim allowed herself a smile. If she was nervous, she was hiding it exceedingly well. Then I noticed a big guy, who looked like he could handle himself, taking a seat at the table next to us. He completely ignored us as he sat back and started to scan the room. I looked at Kim, and saw that she was studying me intensely.

"Right then, Mr Storm, you want to come with me?"

It wasn't really a question, and I wasn't going to make it difficult anyway. She wanted to talk somewhere else, which was fine with me. I just wanted to know exactly how much she knew. I got up.

"After you,"

I glanced at the big guy. He didn't look at me, just at Kim as she gave him a nod of acknowledgement.

"Follow me," Kim instructed, as she moved towards the exit.

In the car park Kim got into the back of a dark grey BMW 7-series saloon with tinted rear windows. I looked in the front and noticed someone was behind the wheel: a woman in her early thirties, another fit and capable type, dressed in black with shiny black hair. She glanced over at me with a cold expression. The rear window came down and Kim spoke to me.

"Join me in the back, Mr Storm." The window went up.

I took a moment to survey the scene; nothing around triggered any suspicion. It was just another busy day in a hospital car park. The big guy who'd followed us scanned the car park too. He didn't look at me, and appeared completely calm, emitting a professional vibe. My gut instinct told me this guy knew what he was doing, and that he would be a challenge if it came to it. Nonetheless, I was certain I could take him out if I had to. But I wasn't here to challenge him – or her for that matter. I just wanted information, and she allegedly wanted to give it me. I got in the back of the vehicle. The scent of expensive perfume greeted me as I made myself comfortable. The big guy came over and leaned against my door whilst continuing to scan the car park.

Kim looked over and smiled, saying, "Ivan is here for my protection, and that alone." Then she pointed to the driver's seat, "And this is my sister."

The driver didn't acknowledge me, though our eyes met briefly in the rear-view mirror. The family resemblance was unmistakeable: sharp facial features, tanned lush skin tone, dark eyes. The sisters were strikingly beautiful, no doubt about it. I turned my attention to Kim.

"I understand. Let's get to the point. Is this about my daughter?"

My voice gave evidence of my growing frustration. I'd jumped through enough hoops for her now. It was time to get down to business. The colour appeared to drain out of Kim's face.

"Yes, Mr Storm, but you've got to hear me out first. Deal?"

"Okay, but understand this: your muscle mountain out there won't be enough to restrain me if this is some bogus set up."

I held her eyes, and kept my tone calm and measured, but my face said it all. Kim nodded, she fully understood the implications of my words.

"I understand, Mr Storm. Believe me, I've got enough enemies as it is; the last thing I need is to add you to the list."

I didn't reply – just gave her some time.

She cleared her throat and continued, "I watched the media conference yesterday, and it broke my heart, what's left of it anyway." Her laughter was tired and full of bitterness. "Seeing the pain in your wife's face touched something inside me, and I decided, for once, to do the right thing."

She thought Claire was my wife, I didn't correct her, it didn't matter. She shook her head.

"You see, I had a long-term affair with Aaron David Cantor. I am talking years. I lived a lie, believing that he loved me and would, when the time was right, split from his wife and make us official. But he loved somebody else, and it wasn't his wife."

She paused, her eyes welling up with tears. When she spoke again, it was to her own tormented soul. It was like I wasn't there.

"But I loved him. Loved him enough for both of us, so I thought. Then even when it became apparent that we'd never be together, I continued to cling on to the lie. For some reason I couldn't let it go. That made me angry – furious in fact – with myself. I'm a strong person, intelligent and smart. I'm an international business leader and one of the biggest importers of illegal drugs into the UK. Yet for years I've devoted myself to this callous and soul-less man. And now I don't know why."

The part about her being an illegal drugs importer took me by complete surprise. She didn't seem to care, and just continued talking, more to herself than to me, or so it seemed. I knew better than to interrupt, she would get to the part relevant to me in due course. The background would be helpful in any case.

"So, on Saturday evening, I waited for him to lie to his wife yet again, and come over to me. He arrived drunk, and in a foul mood. David doesn't normally drink, it's out of character, you understand. But he was very drunk. I tried to make the peace, I knew he'd been at Ariella's house earlier that day, but I didn't want to know about that. Then he became mean, started taunting me about me loving him, when in fact he loved Ariella and had done for years ..."

She paused for a moment, cleared her throat and continued, "The heartless swine ... he wouldn't leave it alone. Just continued to tell me how he'd killed her husband – his own brother – to clear the way. And then when that wasn't enough, he engineered the kidnapping of Chloe to make Ariella come running to him for help. If she was broken with nowhere else to turn, surely ... but then that didn't even work – she wasn't interested in his help."

The hair was standing up on the back of my neck. I sat, frozen, listening to this crazy story about this monster. The tears were now rolling down Kim's face. She looked over and shook her head again. I kept silent, I didn't know what to say, but I knew I wanted her to continue.

"He was raging about you. Ariella had mentioned a couple of weeks earlier that she wanted to approach you, and David had tried his hardest to talk her out of it, but the more he tried the more committed she became." Kim paused again.

Although I could see where this was going, I needed her to tell me straight. My heart was racing but my mind was clear, absorbing everything.

"I told him to shut up, but he wouldn't. He followed me around the house telling me how he had arranged for your oldest kid to be taken, making sure you wouldn't work on Chloe's case. He'd done it before and had got away with it, so he figured he could do it again. He kept on laughing. Animal! And the realisation hit me that I'd spent years being in love with an absolute monster."

She suddenly stopped speaking, staring at me with surprise on her face, as if she'd just noticed that I was there. But I had been preoccupied too. My mind was racing to process what she'd told me. I felt like I'd been in the boxing ring, groggy and punch drunk. That cold-hearted, self-important, stuffed shirt had taken my little girl. What a villain. The hatred inside of me exploded, and I had to work hard to control my rage.

"Why are you telling me this?" I finally asked, my voice sounding detached, even to my own ears.

Kim held me in her gaze for a long time before she replied, "Because I just had to. For once, I'm doing something right. And I guess ... I owe it to you."

"Owe it to me?"

"Your brother, Douglas, I corrupted his soul."

"What?" I spluttered, in disbelief.

"He works for me, has done for years."

It made sense I guessed, Douglas' police salary hadn't been sufficient to cover his lifestyle for years. I knew the money from his wealthy wife had been cut off a long time ago, but the police weren't aware of that situation, and that had probably saved him from investigations by Internal Affairs. The smoke screen provided by his wife's wealth had made it possible for him to drive around in a BMW M5 as well as enjoying the other features of his lavish lifestyle. I was pretty sure that Eleanor's family detested the embarrassment of being linked to a dirty copper more than they detested Douglas himself. They wouldn't shop him in, but somebody had.

"Who are you people?" I asked.

"Crooks, for the want of a better word. We pretend that we're not, but that's precisely what we are."

"Ariella too?"

"Well, she is a genuine art dealer, and good at it too. She pretends to be my boss and ignores my other activities. It's a good arrangement – or has been for years." She paused, as if taking stock, before continuing. The tears had dried up, she just looked sad.

"Victor was a good guy though, he had his flaws like all of us, but his heart was in the right place. However, he couldn't stomach the business anymore; he was looking for a way out and that spooked David. Basically, that was his death sentence."

"And now he's coming after you?"

Kim looked over at me sharply, her tears had gone, and fire had returned to her eyes.

"That's right ... See, I've got resources, Mr Storm but they're small in comparison to David's. There's more money in shady international arms deals than in illegal drugs trafficking."

"Why haven't you run away, why haven't you boarded a flight to somewhere far away?"

She smiled and shook her head. "Because it isn't as easy as that," she replied.

"No, because you want me to fix this for you ..." My words hung out there for a moment.

"Well, you've got an incentive, a stronger incentive that anybody else I can think of. And you Storm boys are something else. Douglas told me about you, and I must say you appear to be the right calibre to go up against David and his henchmen." She paused and leaned over, her presence was almost overwhelming.

"But, maybe I'm wrong?"

I didn't reply at first; my anger had been reignited. I wasn't here to play a part in her game. I was only interested in getting my girl back. I cleared my throat before stating my position.

"Whatever scenario you're planning, I'm not interested. I just want my little girl back."

"I know, but getting your girl back might fix my problem too."

She had a point, and I decided to let it slide. This wasn't the time for moral integrity, but only for hard-nosed pragmatism.

"What do you know about the kidnapping of my girl?"

"Only what I've told you. You've got to get to David and make him talk."

"What kind of security does he have?"

"The best there is. His security chief is a former Mossad guy, Michael Adler. He's an efficient killer."

I remembered that guy, he'd been my contact on a sensitive job I'd done for the firm a couple of years ago. He was a silent, slick type, menacingly effective. 'An efficient killer', I could believe it!

"Right, I know of him. He's still around?"

"Yes, he's one hundred per cent loyal to David, and utterly ruthless."

I nodded, this was it; I believed what Kim had told me, it rang true, and besides I couldn't see what she could possibly gain by setting me up. However, it was obvious what she could gain from my taking David out; it didn't matter to me. If that was a side-effect, then so be it. She would owe me. I was going after an enemy of a calibre that I'd never previously confronted. This guy had resources and capabilities at a level that I hadn't been up against before. More than likely, he wouldn't have been directly involved in the kidnapping, it would've been outsourced.

"You know a guy called Jason Stewart?" I asked.

"No, but I know Douglas had dealings with him – in what capacity I don't know, nor do I want to know. Just one more thing that you should know: the kidnapping of your daughter wasn't as well planned as the kidnapping of Chloe. David told me that, just before his drunken collapse."

"What happened to Chloe?"

My words hit Kim like a rapid sequence of punches. Her face drained of colour again. She gazed out of her window before she replied.

"I don't know, David never said, but what do you think?"

I swallowed – she was dead – her little body buried somewhere, never to be found.

FIFTEEN

AS I SAT IN MY CAR thinking over what I'd been told, I realised that I needed help. I took out my mobile and called Petite.

"Hugo, how are you?" Her voice was full of concern.

"Right, I know who took Emily. It's that pompous, stuck-up, so-and-so, brother-in-law of Ariella Cantor: Aaron David Cantor. It was diversion tactics, designed to sabotage my investigation of the Chloe Cantor kidnapping."

"What do you need?" Petite was right down to business – no messing about.

"I need your help. First, I need a piece, then I need your online wizardry."

"I'll make some calls, you'll have a piece within two hours max. Do you need a heavy tool too and maybe a silencer?"

Sometimes I wondered which of us was better connected; Petite sure had a wealth of useful contacts in the shadow world.

"Yeah, both, can you make the heavier tool a sniper rifle."

"Right, I'll try, but can't guarantee on that one. The smaller piece and the silencer won't be a problem. Now you want me online – how fast?"

"As fast as possible. Tell Helena to take the kids and head north, use cash only and stay off the grid for the next few days."

"She wants to speak to you, Hugo."

I couldn't really say no. Helena deserved to hear this from me. I was heading into danger here; the possibility that I might not survive was real.

"Of course, is she there?"

"Just a minute."

I waited, I heard the low voices of Petite and Helena, but I couldn't quite make out what they were saying. In the background I could also hear the kids; they were having a riot by the sound of it. Their innocent joy made me smile, but a sad smile. I prayed that I could bring Emily back to that. That one day she would have the joy return to her voice too.

"Hugo, darling what's going on?" Helena's voice was intense and laden with worry.

"I know who took Emily and I'm going after him."

"Yes, Petite said," she hesitated, "You don't want to contact the police, no?"

"No Helena, this guy will claim innocence and he will walk. He's very well connected. I don't have any solid evidence; my source won't talk to the police. If Emily's still alive, she won't be for long if this animal is brought in by the police ... I need to go after him myself and make him talk. There's no other way." I paused, my words were frank and to the point.

Helena took a few moments to reply, she was digesting what I'd told her.

"You're right, Hugo. You do what you have to do to get Emily back. I love you – we love you."

Her voice was breaking up. It was as though she was talking to me for the very last time – saying goodbye.

"Listen, I'll be fine, and I will get Emily. You must believe that ... for me, if for no other reason. You've got to stay strong and take the kids away without me. I'll contact you as soon as it's safe to resurface. Can you do this for me – for us – Helena?"

I needed her to remain on an even keel; the little ones were completely dependent upon her.

"Yeah, sorry. You can trust me, Hugo."

"Good, I know that, always knew that. And I love you too. I've got to go, but can you put Petite back on before I do?"

"Will do. Go and get Emily!"

Her voice sounded strong and determined again. I was pleased about that. As for me, I felt detached from the turmoil within, and I was grateful for that. That's how I needed to be now, sharp and tuned.

"Love you, darling, give the crew a kiss each from dad."

Helena had already disengaged, and I could hear the hushed voices in the background. It sounded like it was Helena and Petite talking logistics. I was blessed with the people who mattered in my life. When everything turned nuclear, they fought themselves through the initial mayhem and became solution-focused.

"Right Hugo, I've made some calls, and your piece will be available in Edinburgh with a silencer. I'm afraid the bigger tool will be more difficult to produce."

"Never mind, I'll make it work with the pistol and the silencer. Just call off the search for the bigger tool. It might filter back to the police, and I certainly don't need that just now."

"Copy that, Hugo. I also rang Aaron David Cantor's office and he is there right now."

"You spoke to him?"

"Yes, I've never spoken to him before, so he didn't suspect. Anyway, I used my southern English voice, presented myself as a reporter researching a feature on Scotland's international businessmen. Guys like that have big egos – most can't resist having them stroked."

I laughed out loud. It felt good to laugh, cleared my head and reset my brain.

"Good one. I like it. Now send me an encrypted message with instructions about picking up the piece. And when do you think you'll be online?"

"In twenty minutes. I'll send the message within the next minute though."

"Good. I'm heading towards Edinburgh right now'" I flipped the gear lever into reverse.

"You got a plan?"

"I'm working on it. The drive will give me chance to formulate one. Stay close to your mobile okay!"

"I'll have it on me at all times, Boss."

"Right, call you soon." With that, I terminated the call.

I'd already begun to consider my approach. I needed to get hold of David straight away. No mucking about, just nail the guy and make him talk. My gut instinct told me Emily was still alive, but the window of opportunity would close sometime this evening. That might've been wishful thinking, but I just felt that she was out there somewhere, holding on ... but for how much longer I couldn't say. I floored the accelerator, navigated away from the hospital and headed towards the M9. I hadn't asked about McGregor, who I presumed was getting angry since I hadn't checked in with him yet. But that was just tough. Neither had I asked about Douglas. I couldn't allow myself to wonder about his fate. Now was not the time to be distracted.

I joined the M9 motorway and sped towards Edinburgh forcing myself not to go too fast. The last thing I needed was to be pulled over by a Police Scotland traffic car. As I settled in for the drive I started thinking about how to get to David. One option would be to confront him at his office. That would be difficult – nearly impossible really – as getting away safely had to be considered. A second possibility would be to grab him in the street, but that wouldn't be the best plan. It could get messy quickly since I was planning to do it myself, and there were a lot of police patrols in Edinburgh. Murphy's law dictated that one of these would likely be close by. Finally, there was his home, I could surprise him there. However, I didn't know where he lived, and what kind of security he had. I would have to learn the layout etc. I knew he had kids, which made it even more difficult. I wouldn't want to create a drama in front of them; the sins of their father weren't their fault. If I chose that option, I'd have to wait until he got home, whenever that might be. None of these ideas carried much promise.

I needed to lure him to a place where he would relax and where nobody would intervene when I put the screws on him. A thought suddenly popped into my head, and I had to smile to myself – it was a pretty good idea, even if I said so myself. I hit the steering wheel in excitement. That was it, he would go there, probably race there, if Ariella asked him. According to Kim, Ariella was the one he had wanted for years. She needed to be on board – would she be? I wondered. It depended upon whether she believed the rather incredible story of what David, her brother-in-law, was capable of. I didn't have much time to convince her, but I had to. I needed him at Ariella's house, alone and unsuspecting – he couldn't know that I would be there.

Ariella had to be calm when she asked him to come over, too overt; and a guy like David would be suspicious. I realised there were many elements that could sink this plan faster than the iceberg sank The Titanic, but it was the best I could think of.

"Here goes," I said to myself, and rang Petite.

"Yes, Hugo."

"You set up yet?" I asked.

"Yes, I am. What do you need?"

"I need Ariella Cantor, and I need to speak to her in confidence on the phone. Can you make that happen?"

If anybody could do that it would be Petite, she had the undeniable talent of getting people to do what she wanted them to. I too had that ability, but Petite was without doubt superior to me in that department.

"I'll make that happen, Hugo. Let me get to work."

"It needs to happen soon – as in the next ten minutes!"

"Got it," Petite said, and ended the call.

I drove on, whilst pondering over my next moves. The big one was how to get David to talk. I knew if I got hold of him, I'd have to be willing to go all the way. Niceties would not cut the mustard with an animal like him. My mood echoed the darkening, steel-grey sky so typical of Scotland. I would do whatever I had to; the gloves were off! My mobile buzzed, and I used the hands free to answer.

"Ariella's in her office awaiting your call," Petite said. I could hear her tapping on a keyboard. "I've hacked David's office security system. He's in his office too, in a meeting with a bunch of banker types."

"He's got CCTV in his own office?" I asked in amazement. That was a surprise, a guy like him liked to watch others, not be watched himself.

"It's a closed system, not linked to the rest of the office CCTV system. I guess he's got it to make sure nobody snoops around there at night and when he's not there. Unfortunately for him the system's online, and while it's got some impressive firewalls, they're not impressive enough."

"Well Petite, remind me not to upset you in future!"

"You'll be so lucky, Hugo. Now you gonna call Ariella? She's waiting."

"I'll do it right away. I'll call you right back."

I terminated the call and quickly searched for Ariella's number, focussed and pressed dial.

"Hello, Ariella Cantor speaking." The lush, guarded voice filled my car.

"Hello Ariella, it's Hugo Storm. Thank you for taking my call."

"Hugo, what can I say – I'm devastated to hear what's happened to Emily. Do you have any news?"

Her guard appeared to have vanished, which I took as a good sign. I needed her to be friendly at the least, because what I was planning to tell her later today would shatter her world completely.

"Thank you. Yes, I have a lead, a very strong lead, which I need to discuss with you face-to-face – and only with you. This needs to be done in absolute confidence between the two of us only." My voice carried the urgency and desperation I genuinely felt. She didn't reply immediately, but when she did speak the ghost of her missing daughter was present in her voice.

"Are you telling me that the disappearances of my daughter and your daughter are linked?"

"Yes!" I replied emphatically.

"When can we meet? Where are you?" She didn't waste time getting straight to the point.

"What if we meet at your house in an hour?" I suggested.

"Yes, let's do that."

"Good. I urge you not to tell anybody of this meeting, not even your brother-in-law. You also need to send your house assistant home. Can you do that?"

The moment of silence stretched out as Ariella considered what I'd requested. She was an intelligent woman; did she harbour any suspicions about her brother-in-law I wondered? From what Kim had told me, she didn't, but that wasn't necessarily the truth. Ariella came across as an individual who kept her cards close to her chest. This astute observer of human nature and clever operator of complicated life situations listened more than she spoke.

"Don't worry, I won't tell anybody, and we will be alone."

Her voice was measured and strong. I wondered what she was thinking. Time would tell.

"Great. I'll see you at your house within the hour."

"Goodbye, Hugo. See you in an hour," she said and hung up.

Could I trust her? I allowed myself to consider this for a moment. I decided that I had no choice. But unless she was somehow involved in the kidnapping of her own daughter, which seemed ridiculous, I was pretty sure I could.

I was fast approaching Edinburgh as I speed-dialled Petite again.

"Go ahead, Hugo."

"Right, it's set up. I'm meeting her at her house in under an hour. Have you sent me the details for picking up the tools?"

"Yes, I have. He's expecting you. Just call the number in the message – say 'blue horseshoe loves yellow horseshoe', and he'll come out to meet you. And by the way, do you want a briefing on the bigger picture?"

I memorized the silly code sentence, but then hesitated to answer; I wasn't quite sure if I wanted to know the bigger picture just now. But common sense prevailed, and I answered in the affirmative.

"Well, Douglas is still missing. Police Scotland are now actively looking for him and McGregor is going berserk as he wants you too. Claire wants to speak to you as well."

It was as expected really, I'd been off the radar for about twenty hours now. But I couldn't speak to McGregor at that moment. He was a very experienced investigator; possibly he would be able to extract something from our conversation and somehow intercept me. And Claire – poor Claire – she could derail me here; I couldn't allow either to happen. Not right now.

"I can't deal with any of that now. Can you hold them off?"

"Yes, McGregor is huffing and puffing something crazy, but what can he do to me? They don't know where I am. What about Claire though, she's really hurting, Hugo. Do you want me to speak to her, I'll make sure all your operational details are secure."

"Yes, speak to her. Thank you. Tell her I'll call her later."

"Right then, I will. Call me any time. Stay safe."

"Cheers."

I was reading the message from Petite. My gun contact was situated at an independent car dealership, a very posh, premier outlet, dealing with exotic and expensive second-hand cars on the western outskirts of Edinburgh. I knew where it was, and headed towards it.

Within twelve minutes I had parked outside the dealership in question, and called the number. Someone answered quickly, I recited my code sentences, and the guy on the other end played the wrong-number game and quickly hung up. It took another seven minutes, with me getting restless before this smart-looking guy appeared. He was carrying a black leather bag, and he looked around as he walked through the front car court. I got out and made sure that he saw me. As he approached I recognised him: it was Will Williams, Petite's cousin, successful hustler and self-declared playboy. I liked the guy and his swagger, always made me chuckle. But I wasn't in the mood for that now and hoped he'd keep his mouth shut. He did: he knew the consequences would otherwise be devastating, and not only from me. Petite would fight to get to the front of the queue. I got back in the car and lowered my window. Will came over and stooped down.

"Hi there, Hugo. Here you go," he said as he handed me the bag.

"Thanks, Will. See you later," I said and put the bag on the passenger seat.

Will stepped back and nodded to me as I drove away. His normal cocky smirk was noticeably absent. I was driving towards Ariella's house, adrenaline pulsing through my body, tooled-up, and emotionally ready for what lay ahead.

SIXTEEN

I KNEW ARIELLA HAD a big beast of a vehicle, complete with a chauffeur, to drive her around most days, but for pleasure and privacy she used a sporty thing, namely a Porsche Cayman. It was that particular vehicle that was parked in her drive as I pulled up outside her fancy house. I had circled the block a couple of times just to see if there were any suspicious cars parked nearby but none were to be seen. Sitting in my car, I studied the house for a moment. Although the blinds were down and the curtains drawn I could see light, which must've been coming from the upper floors, as the ground floor was sheltered behind a substantial brick wall. I checked the pistol and the magazine, fed a bullet into the chamber and made sure the security was on. Then I clipped the holster onto my belt and dropped the silencer into my right-hand jacket pocket.

Getting out of the car, I took my time to check both directions. There was nothing out of the ordinary to be seen, if one could call this street in any way ordinary, with its lavish houses and expensive cars parked outside. Satisfied that, so far, no nasties were waiting, I quickly walked up to the metal gate and rang the bell. I had to ring it a few times before Ariella answered.

"Yes Hugo, come on in."

There were a couple of cameras covering the entrance, so I flipped my thumb up to the one I assumed she'd be using. The walk-in gate buzzed and unlocked. I quickly entered. Ariella was waiting for me at the front door, dressed in a black and grey trouser suit, looking very much like the business woman that she was. She didn't smile as I approached, just gestured for me to follow her inside. The house was quiet; there were no signs of the housemaid or anybody else.

"Relax, Hugo. There's only you and I here. That is what you wanted, isn't it?" She'd noticed me scanning the house as I followed her to the lounge.

"Indeed Ariella, that is what I wanted."

She stopped in the middle of the room and pointed to the seat that I'd sat in when I'd been there on Saturday. Saturday! That seemed so long ago; it was hard to believe that so much could have happened since then.

"Would you like a drink?" she asked, gesturing towards the refreshments that were set out on a glass tray.

"Coffee please, black with two sugars if possible," I replied and smiled.

She poured a coffee, dropped a couple of sugar cubes into it and brought it over to me. I felt the slight tremor in her hand as I took the cup from her. She smiled tightly, and hastily retreated to the chair opposite mine. I took a sip of my drink and looked over at her.

"Thank you." I said and placed the cup on the small, conveniently-placed table.

"So, if you don't mind Hugo, could you please tell me what is going on?"

I sensed the tension within her as she used all her strength to stay calm and collected. She knew this was very important, but the waiting was breaking her spirit. I'd rehearsed several scenarios in my head as I'd driven here. All of them revolved around how to break this shocking news to Ariella, and how to enlist her help in luring

David here. I'd settled on being up-front and straight to the point – brutally so. Determinedly, I cleared my throat.

"This might be difficult for you to believe, but you must hear me out."

"Of course, Hugo. Please, tell me."

"Okay. I believe that your brother-in-law, David, killed your husband, then kidnapped your daughter and then kidnapped my daughter." I looked directly at her, hoping to gauge her reaction. At first, she didn't respond, just kept tapping the fingers of her delicate right hand on her left knee. Was she not surprised? I decided to continue.

"Have you seen or heard from Kim Monteith since Saturday?"

She looked at me sharply, her dark eyes drilling into me, giving nothing away.

"No I haven't, but Kim is a busy lady," she finally replied.

"Well, I spoke to her today, and what she told me was, frankly, shocking."

Ariella's eyes remained on me, her body frozen still, her fingers now in a tight fist.

"What do you know about David?" I continued probing.

"Other than that he's an obnoxious, know-it-all snob, and that he had an affair with Kim for years, probably not as much as I should." She had chosen her words carefully and delivered them with great feeling. I raised my eyebrows in response. She nodded, and continued.

"Oh, I knew – but Kim is something far more than my business manager. We pretend, when it suits her, that I'm her boss, but trust me that is not how this really works." She lowered her gaze and I saw her efforts to keep her self-control.

"Explain how you know that David killed Victor and then took our girls." Her voice now started to crack. Her words seemed to show that she didn't doubt the truthfulness of this awful situation, but her eyes reflected a hope that it wasn't really so.

"Victor wanted out, and it seems that David has wanted you forever. I don't know which of those factors was the trigger – possibly a combination of both – but something tipped the scale in any event. That's how Victor died, but you continued to keep David at a distance, which wasn't in his plan. And then you wanted to re-open Victor's case, which led to Chloe's disappearance. I guess David had calculated that if you were broken, you'd run to him ..." I paused and cleared my throat. The darkness in the man was terrifying.

"Then you wanted me to search for Chloe and that led to Emily's disappearance." I just about managed to say that without breaking down.

"Heartless animal!" Ariella exclaimed in a hoarse voice, tears flowing down her drawn, pale face. I nodded agreement, fighting to keep my own emotions in check. We sat in silence for a while.

"What now?" Ariella's voice was hardly more than a whisper.

"I believe my Emily is still alive, but not for much longer. I need to get hold of David!"

Ariella's look told me that she knew what I was saying.

"If I get him here, will you make him tell the truth?"

I involuntarily clenched my teeth and fists. Ariella recognised my rage.

"I'll get him here, Mr Storm – right away – leave it to me! Can you make him tell me about Chloe? Where her body is ..." Her lips started trembling and the tears returned. I reached out with my hand and she grabbed it.

"Yes, I'll make him talk!" I promised, swallowing hard. The anger inside me had taken hold and had forced away the grief. I was glad – I would need that anger to carry me through this ordeal. Ariella freed her hand from mine and got up. She swayed a little, so I rushed to support her. Her perfume was delicate and rich. She held my hand for a moment and looked up at me. I realised how fragile she was.

"Thank you, Hugo. I just felt a little light-headed there. Now, let me get David." As she turned, I let go of her hand and remained standing.

"You okay, Ariella?" I asked as she walked unsteadily over to her handbag, which lay on a cabinet.

"No, I am not okay, but don't worry – I won't faint," she said and gestured for me to stay put. She retrieved her phone, came over and sat down again. "Now, where might David be?"

"Just a moment," I said and got out my mobile. I quickly called Petite to ask if she still had eyes on David. She confirmed that he was at his office behind his desk. I could see that Ariella was impressed as I thanked Petite and terminated the call.

"You are a man of resources, Hugo," commented Ariella as she started to call David's office number.

I lifted a hand. We hadn't discussed what she would say, but Ariella had it under control, or so I hoped. It was too late anyway, as David answered. Ariella played her part well, saying that she needed to see him immediately at her home, as Kim had called and made threats against her. Ariella also told him that Kim was just about to meet me in Glasgow. I was impressed by her acting, she sounded sincere and very convincing to me. Ariella ended with a plea for David to come to her house alone, straight away. She then picked out a cigarette from a silver case lying on the table, lit it with a gold lighter and took a long draw.

"You think that will work?" she asked, looking directly at me.

"We'll soon find out," I replied and quickly got Petite back on my mobile.

"Ariella just called him. What's he doing now?" I asked.

"He's suddenly in a hurry!" Petite's voice sounded quite excited.

"Is he using any phones?" I asked.

"No, he's shutting down his computer and locking his desk. The man is on the move; he's leaving his office. I've hacked the general CCTV system too. Do you want me to follow him for as long as possible?" Petite asked.

"Yes!" My big question was, would he arrive alone, or would he bring muscle? The latter situation would complicate matters. Petite gave me a running commentary as David left the office in a hurry. The good news was that he got into his own car, a sleek Porsche 911, and fired it out of the underground garage. I told Petite to stay close to the phone.

Ariella had heard Petite's comments. "He is coming, and he's coming alone," she confirmed.

"Yes, we need to prepare. You know this is going to get nasty, yes?" I looked her straight in the eyes. Her face was as hard as stone, and what could only be described as pure hatred radiated from her dark eyes.

"Yes, I expect nothing less. Make the beast talk, Hugo!"

I considered her for a while, making sure she was genuine. Then I looked around the room.

"Meet him at the door and bring him in here. I'll take him as he steps inside. You keep your distance from him, okay. If he has a gun out when he arrives, you retreat and let me know. Okay?"

"I hear you, Hugo."

"Good, now I need knives and whatnot. Where's your kitchen?" I asked. Ariella pointed me in the right direction. I calculated we had between twenty to forty-five minutes, depending on traffic. Being on the safe side I decided to work on the premise of twenty minutes. I found what I needed and went into the hall. There were several doors leading off, one of which was on the right side with a small window to the front of the house. It would take me five long steps to come out and take him down from behind. Full on aggression. Then I would quickly tie up his arms and legs using plastic straps. I told Ariella my plan, and we waited. The minutes went by at a snail's pace; at least that was how it felt. I was usually a patient guy, but this was different.

SEVENTEEN

THE CLOUDS HAD GATHERED above, dark and menacing. A certain chill appeared to grip the city of Edinburgh. I stood in the dark of the cloakroom and looked out of the small window, my heart was pounding, and the veins were thumping in my neck. All colour seemed to have melted away from the world outside. It was getting late, but Aaron David Cantor had still not arrived, so Ariella phoned again, only for the call to go straight to his voicemail. Petite had worked her magic, but to no avail. David, I couldn't help but think of him as David, appeared to have disappeared.

"Give it another half hour!" I encouraged myself, willing him to appear through the gate. I felt terrible, utterly terrible. Had he somehow smelled the trap and was now busy disposing of my daughter's dead body? Chloe was long gone, but I tried to cling to the hope that Emily could still be alive. That hope was slipping though; a voice inside my head told me she was gone. The nausea in my stomach became acute and I worried that I might vomit. My hands were clammy and sticky. I took a couple of deep breaths and steeled myself, repeating the mantra: "Keep it together. Don't think – just wait."

"Come on you coward, show yourself. She loves you, she needs you!" I whispered under my breath, trying to keep my focus away from those terrifying thoughts of a dead Emily buried in cold soil. A tentative knock on the door sounded awfully loud in my ears. I quickly opened it, causing Ariella to step back in surprise. The look on my face had clearly shocked her; I could see the fear in her eyes.

"What shall we do, Hugo? It's been two hours now."

Ariella bit her lip and wrung her hands together in pure anxiety. She looked as white as a white sheet of paper.

I couldn't make any useful suggestions, so I simply said, "We have to wait – just a little longer – he'll come."

My words sounded so hollow, even to my own ears. I could see from her expression that she was trying to believe me. I reached out and gently laid my right hand on her fragile shoulder. She had to stay strong; I needed him inside the house before I could grab him. He was a predator, he could probably smell a trap from afar.

"Listen, stay strong, compose yourself, he will come, and soon."

The last remaining part of me that believed those words was losing the battle against increasing doubt. Nevertheless, I managed to sound convincing as Ariella breathed deeply and composed herself.

"Okay Hugo. I trust you," she said giving me a long look.

I kept my game face on.

"Good, now wait in the living room. I'll keep this door ajar. Remember to bring him in immediately, and go straight into the living room. Don't kiss or hug him as he enters. Make him follow you."

I gave a little wave, gesturing for her to return to the living room, which she did. I walked quickly back to my position at the window, leaving the door slightly open. It was better that way; I could charge out and overwhelm him, if the coward turned up, that was.

Clearing my head, I ignored the relentless ticking of my wristwatch, marking the slow passage of time, as I kept watch at the window. The minutes ticked away, becoming quarters and then halves of yet another hour. Then, suddenly, I heard a car coming up the street. I could tell it was a sports car; the engine had the snarl of a high-performance vehicle. My whole being went into combat mode, my senses sharpened, and my muscles tensed, ready to explode into action. I couldn't see the car, but I sensed that he was here.

I waited, looking through the window towards the gate, standing at an angle where David wouldn't be able to see me. The light outside and the darkness in the room should've made that impossible anyway, but a smart guy always factors in the 'what ifs' of a situation. The gate bell rang, and I heard Ariella answer the intercom. Her voice was steady and clear, yet gave evidence of sufficient anxiety to fit our arranged scenario.

"David, thank Heavens! Please come in." I knew she was watching him through the camera.

"You alone?" he asked, his voice heavy with suspicion. I'd moved my car further away, but I guessed the guy couldn't help but be suspicious.

"Of course. I've been waiting for you, David. Come in."

Ariella said this with just enough annoyance in her voice to ring true. There were a few seconds of silence before the intercom beeped, as it turned off.

"He's alone," she whispered to me.

I didn't reply; I was watching the guy who had killed my daughter, as he walk decisively towards the house. I felt it in my bones; he had ended her before he came here. I swallowed hard, feeling the fury inside filling every inch of my body. He was scanning right and left, I knew he had his doubts, but the lure of Ariella was drawing him in. Years of unrequited lust and love for her must've been consuming him from the inside out. He suddenly looked at my window. I quickly slid further back into the darkness. Had he seen me? I held my breath and got ready to charge after him if he turned away. There was no way I would let him get away, even if I had to take him down in the street. I was just running through this scenario in my mind when he appeared again in a small section of the window that I could still see out of. He was still coming. Then the door opened, and he stepped into the house.

"I'm here David, in the lounge," Ariella called in a light voice.

Silence. He was on the other side of the door, trying to figure out whether it was a trap. I held my breath again and remained completely still. Was he armed? Did he have a gun pointed at my door? The wood panelling would not stop a bullet. I had my gun up aimed at the door too. But I couldn't shoot. I needed answers, not a dead man.

"David?" Ariella called again.

"Coming!" David replied.

I saw his shadow moving as he walked towards the living room. It was now or never. I exploded into action, charged out of the utility room and against him as he spun around towards me. In the split second before I reached him, I noticed he was wearing gloves and holding a gun with a silencer. He moved quickly, but not quickly enough. I rammed against his body with a classic rugby tackle and grabbed his gun arm whilst smashing him into the door frame of the living room. The impact shattered the glass in the door, and the art on the wall came crashing down. David groaned as his shoulder took the impact, completely winding him and knocking the gun out of his hand. I backed away as he fell to the floor, and looking around quickly, I located his gun. He lay groaning on the floor, in a painful semi-conscious state.

Ariella stepped forward and looked down at him. She noticed his gloves and the gun that I'd retrieved.

"You filthy scum," she spat on him and shouted as she started to move closer, maybe to follow up with a kick. He definitely deserved it, but I didn't want her in any danger.

"Hey, don't get too close. I need to secure him first, okay!"

I shouted a warning as I tried to control my breathing. The action had only lasted a few seconds, but I'd charged at him with everything I had, and then some. Normally, I would've been totally spent after such an effort, but I was running on pure adrenaline, aware that he might recover at any moment; I had to move fast. I bent down and pulled him away from the wall. He was still drowsy, but cried out in pain. As I ripped his coat off I saw why – his shoulder was dislocated. Too bad for him. I didn't care. If he didn't tell me about Emily, that was nothing to what I would do to him. I quickly searched him and then strapped his legs and wrists together with plastic ties, the latter secured at the front of his body to make it easier to position him on a chair. Then I called Ariella over and gave her the guns.

"Keep your distance from him, okay. And unless I say so, don't shoot the filth. We need answers, you agree?"

Ariella took the weapons from me. They looked massive in her hands, but she had a look of determination and rage on her face, so I knew she would guard them well.

"Yes, got it Hugo."

I bent down and lifted David up; he was a substantial guy, but I had super-powers at the moment. Although the pain woke him up, he was unable to fight back because of his injury. I dragged him into the living room, dumped him on a chair in the middle of the room and tied him to it. I stood back and surveyed the scene, before speaking to Ariella.

"I need a bucket of water."

"Just a moment."

Ariella handed me back the guns and I put them on the table, confident that I could pick them up again in seconds. I heard the sound of running water coming from the utility room, and a few minutes later Ariella returned with a very large bucket. It was full of water, and she was struggling to carry it, so I grabbed it from her.

"How worried are you about your carpet?" I asked.

"Not at all worried," Ariella replied, with a look that said she knew what was about to happen.

I launched the bucket of water into David's face. He spat and cursed and cried in pain.

"Wake up David," I said as I grabbed a chair and seated myself in front of him. Not too close, but close enough. He glared at me defiantly, through a wall of pain.

"Scumbag detective! I'm going to have you killed," he snarled and moved, which made his shoulder pain spike. Howling in pain he tried to support his damaged shoulder by holding the affected arm.

"Listen, you animal – this is just the warm up. You will tell me where my Emily is and where Chloe is, and then maybe – just maybe – your suffering will stop. It's up to you!"

I spoke with passion in my voice, as I held him in my stare. I saw the rot in his eyes as he looked back at me. This guy was indeed evil, pure evil. There was no humanity to see in the dark holes that were his eyes. He didn't reply at first, but looked over at Ariella and tried to smile. I knew he was going to say something smart, so I leaned forward and yanked his injured arm. He instantly shot back and cried out in pain.

"Hey, don't you look at her. You look at me and only me. There's no point trying to lie; I know everything. A little bird came calling! Told me everything."

I sat back, watching for his reaction. David managed to pull himself together, and this time I noticed something new in his eyes: fear. He knew I would hurt him, hurt him badly.

"I don't know anything about these girls' kidnappings. That's absurd ... no, no ..."

I ignored his plea, and grabbed his arm again, only this time I yanked it even harder. He managed to lift the chair as he winched in pain and keeled over, only to cause himself still more pain. So much so, that he passed out. It was just as well he was lying on his side, because he then started to vomit.

"Oh no!" exclaimed Ariella.

She was standing at the back of the living room, shaking. Her face was a ghastly white, drained of all colour.

"Look at me, Ariella," I ordered, and she reluctantly met my eyes.

"You don't need to watch this; in fact, it'd be better if you didn't. But whether you do, or you don't, I've got to do this. Do you understand?"

She was about to respond when something caught her eye. She looked straight past me, and her mouth fell wide open. Pure fear was written all over her face. There was somebody there. Somebody was standing at the entrance of the living room. I was still looking at Ariella.

"Well, well, what on earth's going on here?" I heard a male voice ask.

Although the guns were within reach, there was no chance that I'd be able to grab one and turn towards the door without having my brains blown out first. The voice continued, not without a little pompous amusement either.

"You be a smart boy and leave those guns exactly where they are – that is if you want to live."

The disembodied voice spoke English, but with a foreign accent that I'd heard before, though I couldn't quite place it.

"Steady now. I'm not going for the gun," I spoke calmly whilst raising my hands.

"Good. Now what exactly have you two conspirators done to my boss?"

The question was followed by a mean laugh. It suddenly dawned on me – Michael Adler – David's security man and former Mossad agent. I remembered what Kim had said about him: 'efficient killer'. I turned my head and looked at the man who was pointing a gun at me. He was of medium height and medium build, wearing a neat suit, with short black hair and chiselled, tanned facial features; he looked very much like a fit businessman, except for the killer look in his eyes and the gun in his hand. I knew this guy was the real deal: lethal, agile and utterly ruthless. He glanced at his boss without any empathy, and shook his head, but a small grin remained on his lips. His aim was towards me, as he held the gun steadily. Ariella stood frozen to the spot behind me.

"Hugo Storm, that's you, isn't it." he checked, with a widening grin.

"Yes, that's me."

"You did a couple of jobs for me a few years ago. I remember you. I liked how you operate. You have that thing that not many have."

"What thing?" I asked.

"The killer instinct. Shame," he said and laughed.

His obvious enjoyment really bugged me. I didn't reply, I was trying to work out a ploy – something I could do to get hold of a gun and kill this guy before he killed me.

"Well, I came here to help the boss clean up the mess, but I guess it'll take a little longer." He rolled his shoulders and pointed his gun at my face as he said, "Time to die, Mr Storm!"

Two gun shots rang out, and I fell out of my chair. As I landed on the floor another gunshot resounded, but I couldn't feel any impact! Where were the entry wounds? No pain anywhere! I scrambled to my feet. In front of me lay Michael Adler, face down with blood rapidly pooling around his head. What the hell. I looked up and saw a guy standing in the hall, smoke coming from his gun. I did a double-take; it was my brother! It was Douglas.

"Douglas, I thought you were dead," I shouted.

"Hugo – guess most people do. Uh, anyway, might want it to stay that way."

Douglas laughed, showing the gap where his front teeth had once been. He looked awful; his left eye was swollen shut and he had lacerations all across his face. My eyes strayed to his left hand and I saw that it was covered by a bandage. Douglas followed my gaze, shrugged, and explained, "I told them I was left-handed, and they believed me."

"I thought Cameron had you. I was convinced he'd killed you. He was next on my list, after this ..." I gestured towards David, who was still lying on the floor, groaning in pain.

"Yeah, they did have me. I'm sure I was intended for fish food at the bottom of the Forth, wearing concrete shoes. But I woke

up earlier than they expected; their drug-calculation skills are rub-
bish."

I walked over and gave him a big hug.

He whispered quietly in my ear, "Sorry brother. I'm truly sorry."

"Don't be. You're here now," I said as we awkwardly freed ourselves from the hug.

"How did you know?" I asked.

"I talked to Petite and she told me everything. Seems like I got
here just in time." He took a step to the side and pointed at David
on the floor.

"Does he still have his tongue intact?"

"Yes!"

"Right then, you take this nice lady outside, and leave me with
this guy. I promise you, Hugo, you will have Emily soon."

Douglas' voice was deep and sinister. I felt the hair on the back
of my neck stand up.

I shook my head, "No, no, I'm staying. It's my Emily."

Douglas looked disapproving of my insistence, and replied,
"No, you don't need to be a part of this. The only thing you need is
to know where Emily is. What difference would it make for you to
participate in this. None, I tell you. You listen to me, Hugo. Listen
to me, and go outside. You want Emily? Then let me get to work!"

I knew Douglas was talking sense. There was no benefit in my
taking part in torturing this animal. I reluctantly nodded in agreement, and gestured for Ariella to follow me.

"Okay then, Douglas, I'm just outside."

Douglas didn't reply, just stood there staring at his victim.
David was now alert and had heard the conversation between us.
He was looking up at Douglas, and shaking in fear. I grabbed Ariel-
la and we ran out of the house.

EIGHTEEN

I WAS IN MY CAR RACING through the streets of Edinburgh, a Police Scotland traffic car behind me, working hard to keep up. Nothing mattered to me but my destination. I could hear the sirens from other police cars around me, but I could only see where I was driving. The powerful Jaguar was pushed to the limit. The suspension worked furiously to keep the beast on the road, and the engine howled up front as I worked it merciless. I was racing to get to Emily. David had spilled the beans and told Douglas where she was, claiming that both Chloe and Emily were dead. The animal had exclaimed gleefully that Emily was dead, as he suffocated in his own blood in his final moments.

I didn't stop to think, I just drove, racing through the midst of Edinburgh towards the address he'd given. She was in the basement of a detached house in Trinity. I didn't allow myself to think – I just needed to get to her.

Suddenly a police car appeared on my left as I cut through a crossroad. It was a Ford Focus, a much lighter vehicle than my heavy Jaguar. I steeled myself and slammed the wing of my car into it. The police car went into a spin and I almost lost control too, but somehow managed to keep on track. Because of this collision, a horrendous noise was coming from the front left wheel, but I kept going. It wasn't far now. I flung the car into a sharp left-hand turn and found myself inches away from a head-on crash. Behind me a wall of blue lights and sirens filled the early Edinburgh evening. I was almost there, another right-hand turn and the steering wheel felt almost detached. I managed to straighten the car as it swerved, and powered on. On my right was the house, an older, two-storey building with a stone wall and a closed metal gate. I aimed the car towards the gate and floored the accelerator. Two tons of mass hit it and blew it off, as if it were made of paper. I stood on the brakes, but the car crashed into the front of the house anyway. The airbags deployed as I was hurled forwards, the seatbelt trying to hold me back. I almost fell unconscious, but an inner voice urged me to get out and find Emily. The door wouldn't budge to begin with, but I kicked and kicked until it finally swung open. I grabbed the gun that Douglas had given me and scrambled out.

"Stop. Don't move!" A stern voice shouted.

I looked around. The world was spinning, and blood was running down my face from a laceration above my left eye. Somehow, I managed to remain on my feet and focus on the voice. It was a solitary cop, but another two soon arrived. They froze and held their hands out. They'd seen my gun.

"Listen, I'm not going to shoot unless you try to stop me. I'm Hugo Storm, and my daughter is here, in the basement of this house," I shouted as I took a few shaky steps away from the car.

"We know who you are. Are you sure your daughter is here?" One of the cops shouted. They were unarmed, and trying to stay calm, and keep the situation under control.

I realised that I looked like a lunatic, and could only hope they'd believe me. I really didn't want to shoot any of them, but I would if I had to.

"Yes I am. Let me find her, and then you can take me into custody – but not until then."

My hoarse voice was cracking up. I raised the gun. I could taste the blood now, and I felt very dizzy. I wondered how much longer I could manage to stay upright.

"Okay, let's find the basement, but put down your gun," the cop shouted. It was the same one; I guessed he must be the senior officer at the scene.

"No, I keep the gun until I've found my daughter – then you can have it."

The cops looked at each other. Their radios were crackling, and I heard something about the ETA (Estimated Time of Arrival) of the nearest armed police unit. The cop cursed, and silenced his radio, but it was too late; I'd heard the message.

"Listen. I just want my little girl," I shouted, and began walking towards the house.

No lights had come on inside, so either it was empty or those inside were hiding. I didn't care, the entrance to the basement was at the rear of the building. I limped around there. My brother's interrogation had been effective; the given information had so far proved correct. The cops hesitated for a moment, then one of them started to follow me, but the senior guy reached out and tried to pull him back. He shook himself loose and raised his hands into the air.

"Just want to help, mate," he said.

I looked at him for a moment before replying. He seemed sincere, but to make my point I lifted my gun again and said, "Just keep your distance, okay!"

"Will do!" he agreed.

I hurried on, feeling close to collapse. I couldn't allow that to happen, not yet. Then I noticed the opening for the basement and limped towards it as fast I could. It had a metal door with a latch secured by a heavy chain. I examined the chain, and cursed; even a bullet from a pistol would be useless against that. The cop approached me very carefully.

"Hey, let me go and get the chain cutter that we've got in the car."

"Please – no tricks. I just want my girl," I said, holding him in my stare.

"No tricks – promise mate. Just give me a minute."

He turned and ran back. I could hear a heated discussion between him and his colleagues before he reappeared, holding a heavy-duty chain cutter. I stood back and watched, as he grunted noisily from the great effort required to cut through the chain. He lifted the latch and flung the door open.

"Thank you."

I stumbled forward and, as he reached out to steady me, I accidentally dropped the gun. I cursed as he caught me; I was so close – would he let me continue? The world was nothing but a blurry haze now. The cop looked me in the eyes. There was empathy there – I could see it.

"Please," I implored.

"Come on! Let's go!"

He guided me carefully as we navigated the stone steps down into the deep, dense darkness. It was moist and cold in the basement, with a horrible stench that even I, in my diminished state, could smell. The cop brought out a torch and turned it on, methodically searching around the room. I could see that we were standing on a dirt floor, the unevenness of which made me feel woozy. Then the light fell upon a little person, lying on a dirty mattress up against the far wall. My heart immediately went into overdrive, and the haziness of my mind was blown away. I rushed forward and fell to my knees beside the little body. The cop ran after me, keeping the light focussed on the tiny figure. It was Emily! I started to cry uncontrollably, my tears streaming furiously as I gently reached out and felt her cold face. She was lying motionless on her side facing the wall. Her skin was cold to the touch and she showed no reaction as I leaned over her. Was I too late?

"Oh, my goodness." The cop exclaimed from behind me.

I ignored him and gently turned over the lifeless body of my dear daughter, Emily. Her face was dirty, but even in the harsh light I could distinguish shades of pale purple and white. Her lips were blue, and her eyes were shut. I lifted her up and held her close, sobbing, as the bottom fell right out of my world. Then I felt it – a breath against my cheek! Faint, very faint, but a breath nonetheless. I forced my tears away and looked intently at Emily's face, searching for any signs of life. Very slowly, her lips started to move. Miraculously, and almost imperceptibly, a single word was whispered:

"Dad ..."

About the Author

Anton Lindbak was born in Norway. He has lived in Scotland since 2001, finding the wet, cold and dark days much like home. He has more than a decade's experience working in Scottish hospitals emergency departments, and has seen it all. More than anything else, he loves to write crime fiction and has been at it for twenty-plus years. 'A Little Bird Came Calling' is his first crime novel under his own name and he is currently busy writing more Hugo Storm crime thrillers.